NEVER BET YOUR LIFE

GEORGE HARMON COXE

Never Bet Your Life

WILDSIDE PRESS

A condensed version of this novel appeared in American Magazine
under the title of Weapon of Fear.

TO

GEORGIE

AGAIN

NEVER BET YOUR LIFE

The man who was responsible for John Gannon's two suicide attempts arrived at the Seabeach Motel late on a hot Florida afternoon. That night Gannon was killed— after Dave Barnum had strangely passed out at the Club 80. There were motives all over the place, mostly involving money. But then Gannon had been a pretty hard boy, a gambler, a promoter, and more recently in handbooks, and had never lacked enemies. In the beginning Captain Vaughn had considered Dave one of his best suspects. Later, when Betty Nelson narrowly missed being the second victim, Dave knew he would have to find out why before it was too late. This is another of George Harmon Coxe's smooth, satisfactory mysteries. As Lenore Glen Offord said in the San Francisco Chronicle: *"You can hardly call yourself a mystery fan if you've never read any of his stories." And, of course, if you have, you know you'll enjoy this one.*

1

THE MAN who was responsible for John Gannon's two suicide attempts in the weeks immediately following the tragic death of his daughter—an only child who had been, in fact, his only living relative—came to the Seabeach Motel late in the afternoon of a hot April day.

The south-bound bus deposited the visitor at the side of the road, and he waited there inspecting the buildings and grounds until traffic permitted him to cross over. He looked to be about thirty, a tall man, blond and bareheaded. His clothes were expensive; so was the large bag he carried. He seemed in no hurry and took his time inspecting the landscaped oval and the neon sign that nightly proclaimed VACANCY or NO VACANCY, before continuing on to the first unit on the right.

This housed the office and the apartment of George Stinson, the manager, who was working on his accounts and stood up as the door opened, a sandy-haired, bespectacled man clad in a slack suit and sandals. He smiled tentatively as he stepped behind the desk and examined his prospective tenant.

"I believe you have a reservation for Frank Tyler. I wired you yesterday from Boston."

Stinson nodded. "Oh, yes, Mr. Tyler. I have something at ten dollars a day. Number 6." He reached for the registration pad and pen. "If you'd care to inspect it first—"

Tyler cut him off. He said that would not be necessary. He wrote down his name and a Los Angeles address; then glanced up, still holding the card.

"This is the place John Gannon owns, isn't it?"

"That's right."

"He's staying here? . . . Is he around now?"

"I think he is. He was out fishing today but I think I heard him come back." Stinson examined the card and reached behind him for a key. When he had collected the customary one night's rent and the state tax, he led the way outside and handed Tyler the key.

The Seabeach Motel might have been called average for that part of the country, in that it was attractive, clean looking, and well run without having the de luxe features of some establishments that boasted swimming pools, sun decks, and plush appointments. Two long, low, coral-colored buildings, separated by eighty feet of lawn and small palms, stretched back toward the ocean, visible through the trees some two hundred yards away. There were four units in each structure, each with its own car-port opening on the gravel driveway that circled the property. Beyond the driveway on the opposite side, and having its own parking lot, was a neat-looking restaurant called the Coffee Shop, and at the inner end of the rectangular lawn were three additional cottages, each with two doors. Stinson pointed at the one in the middle standing closest to the ocean.

"That's Mr. Gannon's cottage."

"Which door?"

"Well—the right one, though either would do. A friend shares the cottage. A Mr. Barnum."

Dave Barnum witnessed this scene from behind the screen door of the Gannon cottage without thinking about it or even knowing who Tyler was. He leaned against the casing with a half-consumed highball in his hand, a lanky man in his late twenties dressed in dirty white ducks, a T-shirt, and sneakers. He had a wide, easy mouth, a hint of stubbornness in the slant of his jaw, and at the moment his dark-blue eyes were morose and brooding, like his thoughts.

In the beginning, when the senior partner of his law firm had suggested that Dave accompany John Gannon to Florida and stay with him a couple of weeks, he understood that he would have to be a sort of companion-male nurse; what he had not understood was that the job could be so wearing, both on Gannon and himself.

At the moment Gannon did not look as if he needed a nurse. Sitting in the living room behind Dave and talking to Carl Workman, his fishing companion of the past week, he was a stocky, graying man with a florid complexion, a vigorous manner, and a hoarse, flat voice. Physically there was nothing wrong with him; what the doctors were trying to find out was how sound he was emotionally.

So far as Dave knew, Gannon had been a gambler most of his life, a promoter of this and that, including certain black-market operations during the war and, until recently, handbooks. A tough, aggressive man who neither asked for sympathy nor gave it, he had but one chink in his armor: his daughter, Alice.

He had managed to enter her in a good school, had given her everything she wanted as she grew up, only to have her elope the summer before with an actor who had been playing in summer stock on the Cape. For that Gannon never forgave her. As a result the remorse he suffered served only to heighten the shock of her tragic death three months earlier when her husband had driven their car into a tree at high speed. For the first time in his life Gannon found himself up against something he could not take, and his crack-up had been complete.

An alert nurse who grabbed the back of his pajamas kept him from going out an eighth-story window a week after the funeral. Prompt action with a stomach pump saved him the second time, following an overdose of sedative. After that a month in a rest home under medical and psychiatric supervision helped to straighten him out, and finally it was decided that perhaps the best therapy would be to let him do what he wanted to,

since short of confinement and round-the-clock observation there was no way a man could be kept from suicide
if he insisted on carrying it out.

"Outside interests and time will do it," the doctors
said to Dave. "Let him do what he wants to but do it
with him."

Because of a long-standing personal obligation, Dave
had agreed. So had Gannon. And since their arrival a
week before what Gannon wanted to do was golf, fish,
and play some nightly roulette at the Club 80 down
across the county line. On the face of it, it was an ideal
existence, but after four or five days Gannon began to
resent the constant attention. He grew sullen and edgy,
then sarcastic, and finally downright cantankerous.
He kidded Dave in front of others. He introduced
him as his male nurse and addressed him as such to
his face.

Dave took it but now, leaning there in the doorway
and reviewing the past days, he wondered how much
longer he could keep it up. He had been conscientious
in his attention to his job but he felt it was time to call
the office in Boston and tell them that Gannon seemed
to be cured of any suicidal tendencies.

There was also a personal reason why he wanted a
little freedom of his own. Her name was Betty Nelson,
a slender, brown-haired girl with hazel eyes, a forthright, friendly manner, and a complexion marred only
by a small saddle of freckles on the nose that succeeded
somehow in showing through the tan. She managed the
Coffee Shop and Dave was in love with her. . . .

"Nurse!"

The now familiar word cut across his thoughts like a
saw blade, leaving a ragged edge of resentment. He
straightened slowly, watching the blond man who had
recently entered number 6 come out and start toward
the Gannon cottage. He turned, his smile fixed, to find
Gannon sitting back in his chair, legs crossed and an
empty glass in his hand.

"Carl and I would like a refill if you can spare the time."

Dave took the glasses. Carl Workman, sitting on the settee, glanced up. He had been in the Coffee Shop the night of their arrival, and before dinner was over he and Gannon were talking fishing a mile a minute. Since then he had offered very little about his background except to say he was an ex-police detective on vacation and looking for a little business deal that might make him a profit. Apparently in his middle thirties, he had a bronzed, hard-jawed face topped by thinning brown hair, and quick observant eyes which now caught Dave's to show he understood.

"Sure," Dave said. "And I think you're going to have company."

He was in the kitchen when the knock came and he heard Gannon call, "Come in!" The door opened and there was a moment of silence and then Gannon's voice again, hoarse, low, and incredulous.

"Tyler!"

Something in the cadence of that voice brought Dave to the doorway. Frank Tyler stood just inside the room watching Gannon with steady eyes. Gannon had leaned forward, his hands clenched on the chair arms, his feet under him as though he was about to spring. He stayed that way, hands ribbed with tendons, the color draining from his face as the stiffness grew there. Under his brows the eyes were hot and hateful. When he spoke his voice reflected the bitterness in his soul but the accents were quiet, the fury contained.

"What're you doing here, Frank?"

"I came to see you. I flew on from the Coast. Went to Boston first and they told me you were down here."

"Why?"

If Tyler was affected by the hostility of his reception he gave no sign of it. He looked poised, unruffled, handsome except for the weakness about the chin and the mouth, which was small and twisted, like a petulant woman's. He shrugged and spoke as if some fledgling playwright had written his lines.

"I find myself in need of funds."

"So?"

"I thought I'd be on hand the first of the month to collect my share of the quarterly profits."

"Your share?"

"You gave Alice a twenty-five per cent interest in this"—Tyler glanced about—"establishment. She assigned that interest to me. I thought you might want to buy me out, or perhaps a bank would take over my interest."

Gannon's hands were still ridged but he continued to speak in the same terribly quiet way.

"When did she make the assignment?"

"About two weeks before the accident."

"I don't believe it."

"I didn't think you would." Tyler stepped forward, taking a folded sheet from his jacket pocket. "I brought along a photostatic copy of the assignment."

Gannon accepted the paper without moving his gaze. "Dave!" he said, still not looking at it. "See what this says."

Dave glanced at the properly signed and witnessed document, noted the date. When he realized that Tyler was telling the truth he said so.

Gannon heaved himself out of the chair and walked heavily across the room, which served as a living room by day and a bedroom by night. Compared to the other units, it was more spacious, and more richly furnished. It was paneled in pine, had a complete kitchen, and certain built-in features. Dave's quarters, reached by a connecting door, were identical except for the kitchen. The reason for all this was that Gannon had built the cottage himself long before he had any idea of making it a motel, and he had put in things he had needed: a hidden sun lamp in the bathroom, a cabinet for his fishing rods, also hidden behind the paneling, and a wall safe, since he was a man who was accustomed to having considerable cash about. In addition it was the only unit having its private telephone.

Now he stopped at the wall, took a coin from his pocket, and pressed it hard against a certain crack. There was a clicking sound and the panel opened to reveal a safe. He spun the combination, turned the handle, then reached for some keys, one of which unlocked the inner door. When he had pawed through the contents he withdrew a paper and handed it to Dave.

Looking again at Tyler, he said: "I got this land on a trade a long time ago. I put up this cottage and the other two so I'd have a place of my own and space to rent if I wanted to. Three years ago I decided to cash in and make a motel out of the property and I needed a man to run it. George Stinson," he said. "You saw him when you came in. I made a deal so he'd have some interest in the place and I gave Alice an interest too so she'd have a little income of her own. Now you think you can cash in on it, huh?" He glanced at Dave. "Tell him what the original agreement says."

Dave was already reading the document. Finally he looked over at Tyler, knowing now what the older man meant.

"You and Stinson," he said, "are entitled to a quarter of the profits, payable quarterly. But Mr. Gannon owns the property. Only in case of his death or liquidation would either of you be able to cash in on your interest."

Tyler frowned and seemed about to speak but Gannon cut him off. "I'll have a check ready for you the first of the month, Frank," he said. "That'll take care of you up to date. Then I'll tell you what I'm going to do."

He sat back, his grin fixed and the fury all there inside him. Tyler waited, a gleam of anticipation working in his eyes.

"Get me Arthur Williams," Gannon said with a nod to Dave. "The County Bank & Trust. You'll probably have to get him at his home."

Dave looked up the number and put in the call. When the banker answered he identified himself and handed the telephone to Gannon. From then on the conversation was one sided but revealing.

"I've decided to put a plaster on this place," Gannon said. "That's right . . . Yeah, as big as I can get. At least a hundred thousand."

He paused, listened, spoke again in a tone that was blunt, iritable, and, to Dave, familiar.

"What the hell do you mean?" he demanded finally, the color coming back into his face. "This place would bring a hundred and fifty grand at a forced sale, and you know it. . . . Yeah. . . . Sure. I know that. I'll tell Stinson and you can send a man down and go over the books tomorrow. Okay, that's more like it."

He hung up and looked at Tyler, taking his time, contempt in his gaze but triumph too.

"You want to cash in, Frank. Well, I'll tell you how it's going to be. When we start paying interest on that loan there'll be damn little net income left for you to chisel. Now get out!" he said, his voice exploding. "And stay out of my way."

For another moment the blond man stood there, face flushed and sullen looking. Gannon turned toward the kitchen. Workman stood up and moved slowly toward Tyler, an assured, competent-looking figure with a hard, unsmiling face.

"You heard him, buster," he said quietly. "On your way!"

Dave watched them and something about Workman's casual manner impressed him strangely. It came to him then that Workman might be a bad man to cross, and apparently Tyler had the same idea. He backed up a step, shrugged the collar of his jacket in place and, turning, pushed open the door.

Workman watched him cross the lawn. He looked back at Dave; then he grinned. "See you at the club," he said. "I got a date with Betty. If you're real polite I might let her dance with you once."

Dave gave him back his grin, annoyed with the restrictions of his job rather than with Workman. "Thanks," he said dryly. "I'll buy you a drink. I'll buy you a Mickey."

2

THE CLUB 80 was a low, white-painted structure standing well back from the highway. The sign that advertised it was small and conservative but the drive, the parking lot, and the main entrance were thoroughly spotlighted so that the doorman and his assistant could examine each new arrival long before he reached the door.

The food here was excellent, the seven-piece orchestra that played for dancing adequate, as was the singer currently featured, a girl named Liza Drake. This part of the establishment was designed to break even; the profit came from a room at the rear where one could try his luck at roulette or blackjack, provided he passed the inspection of the dinner-jacketed husky who policed the narrow corridor leading from the main room.

John Gannon had been a consistent and regular patron of the roulette tables ever since he had come South. His nightly visits were as much a part of his routine as was his insistence that he be at his bungalow at six in the evening to get the news from station WTCX and at eleven fifteen to get the racing results on WCXM.

On this particular evening Dave Barnum was very happy to get to the club. Dinner at the Coffee Shop had been unpleasant for him because Gannon's foul mood, which had been incited by Frank Tyler, had continued throughout the meal. Dave kept his temper by putting mental cotton in his ears, absorbing the petty criticism of his past conduct, and saying nothing at all about Gannon's dissatisfaction with the present arrangement

and his threats to call the office in Boston and have Dave
relieved. Now, at nine fifteen, with the help of a third
after-dinner brandy, Gannon was finally relaxing in his
corner booth with Dave and Liza Drake.

Liza was a lithe, long-legged girl with raven hair
and dark eyes that were expertly shadowed and wise
beyond her years. Her shoulders were smooth and
tanned, and she had a depth of bosom that gave a quality to her strapless dresses that men admired and most
women envied. These things, plus a forthright self-
reliance and a practiced adaptability, made her an asset
to the club quite beyond the songs she nightly offered
for sale.

In the week that Dave had been coming here he had
grown increasingly grateful for Liza's company. Once
he realized that he could keep track of Gannon simply
by watching the lone entrance to the gambling room,
he had talked with her when she was free and danced
with her when he could. It was a nice arrangement
because each was in love with someone else: Dave with
Betty Nelson and Liza with Sam Resnik, who owned
the club. The difference lay in the fact that Dave had
made very little progress while Liza spoke openly of
marriage and wore an emerald-cut diamond somewhat
smaller than a cuff link to prove her claim.

Now, watching the table across the room where Betty
and Carl Workman were finishing their dinner, Dave
felt again the unaccustomed fluttering at the pit of his
stomach. He was aware that Liza and Gannon were
talking right beside him but he knew nothing of what
was said until someone tapped his arm.

"Why," said Gannon when Dave glanced round,
"don't you go over and ask for a dance?"

Dave felt the flush come. He saw Liza was eying him
amusedly. He looked back at Gannon and grinned.

"All right, I will."

He rose and threaded his way among the couples on
the floor. Then he was beside Betty and she was smiling
up at him in her friendly, gracious way.

"Her coffee'll get cold," Workman said, kidding, when Dave had spoken his piece.

"Order her some fresh," Dave said.

The girl shook her head as she gave him her hand and stood up. She said she'd finished her coffee, thank you, and Workman said to hurry back.

Holding her in his arms as they took the first few steps made Dave feel immeasurably better. It made him forget, temporarily, the regulations and confinement of his job, the recent unpleasantness at dinner. Her hair was soft and fragrant against the hinge of his jaw and presently he spoke, wanting to hear her voice, still a little jealous of Workman, not really worried but phrasing his words with mock concern.

"He's much too old for you."

"Carl?" She looked up quickly to see if he was serious. "He's only thirty-five."

"That's what I mean."

"He's very entertaining," she said, glints of humor in her hazel eyes. "He's a wonderful dancer. Also," she said, "he has loads of free time."

"Yeah," Dave said, and sighed, wondering again how you could fall in love with a girl and at the same time never see her alone.

He had liked her immediately he saw her that first night when they had dinner in the Coffee Shop, not knowing then that she was the manager but assuming that she was the head waitress. He liked her even better the following morning when she came to the beach in her two-piece suit that set off her tanned slenderness and firm young curves.

That was the one morning when John Gannon had been content to stay on the beach, and while he sat under his umbrella with *Morning Telegraph* and pencil, Dave made the most of his free time. At once aware of the girl's unaffected friendliness as he stretched out on the sand beside her, he quickly established a common point of interest when he learned she had been born in Boston.

"In Jamaica Plain, really," she said. "They made my birthday a holiday. April 19."

He'd laughed with her then because April 19 was a holiday peculiar to Boston and its environs, and was celebrated as Patriots' Day, an occasion unknown in other parts of the country.

"1931?" he said, guessing.

"1930."

"Which makes you twenty-two."

"As of last week."

He learned a lot of things in those two hours: that she was an orphan, as he was, that her father, who traveled a lot, had lost his life in a hotel fire when she was seven. About that time her mother had moved to New York where she had found work as a dressmaker, studying secretarial work when she could, and later moving on to establish a residence in a college town so Betty could take advantage of the small residential fees. With her mother's help and some scholarship aid, she had been able to earn her degree in home economics and, through the alumnae bureau, had found this job at Seabeach, her first.

She spoke easily of all these things and it came to Dave as he sprawled beside her that there was a lot more to this girl than an unaffectedly pretty face and a nice figure. Even then it occurred to him that if things worked out this might be the girl for him, and when it came time to leave he wanted most of all to ask her for a date that night until, thinking of John Gannon, he knew he could not keep it.

And so he had looked forward to another morning like this, and when it came Gannon had golf on his mind and there was only time for a quick dip and no time for talk. Then, after lunch, she had issued an invitation of her own. A college friend of hers lived in Boothville, a town twelve miles north, and there was to be a beach picnic that evening after the Coffee Shop closed, and would Dave like to go with her?

He had to tell her no without then being able to tell

her why, and since then, though she began to understand the nature of his job, things were never quite the
same. Her friendliness remained but there was reserve
too, the implication being there was little point in
becoming interested in a man who had no time of his
own. Now, remembering all this, he tightened his arm
and she glanced up at him.

"I'm going to change that," he said.

"What?"

"This free-time business. John's getting fed up and I'm
getting fed up. Did you hear him chewing me out tonight in the shop?"

"A little of it. It was disgusting. I wonder how you—"

She broke off, as if aware that it was not her place
to comment on his job.

"You wonder how I stand it. How a man with any self-
respect could put up with him as long as I have." He
spoke without resentment because he felt as she did,
but he had no intention of offering excuses. "Most of the
time I didn't even know what he was talking about. He
said something about a will and getting another lawyer
down to take care of it, and of that I approve."

He hesitated and when she remained silent he said:
"He hasn't been despondent since he's been here. He
doesn't act like a man with suicide on his mind. I'm
going to call the office in the morning and tell them so.
If I can get an okay I'll pull out but"—he grinned down
at her—"not until I've had a couple of days of doing
what I'd like to do."

She stood back as the music stopped. She took his
arm and started back to the table. "That," she said,
"would be nice."

Liza was still in the corner booth when Dave went
back. He had seen Gannon go into the gambling room
while he had been dancing, and now there was a fresh
drink in front of him and Liza announced it was on the
house.

Because he was hot and thirsty, Dave drank quickly.
He gave her a cigarette and a light and leaned back in

his corner, watching the dancers and wondering why
he felt tired until he decided it was the long day on the
water that made him feel that way. Gradually he became aware that Liza was watching him guardedly
and he wondered about that too, but not for long. He
covered a yawn and apologized, and presently Sam
Resnik came along to remind Liza it was time for some
songs.

He put his hand lightly on her bare shoulder as he
spoke, and as Liza glanced up she covered the hand
with her own. Something about the gesture and the
sudden shining look in her eyes spoke so obviously of
her love that the mere fact of witnessing it gave to Dave
a secret pleasure and made him think of Betty.

Liza nodded wordlessly and stood up, straightening
her dress and pulling up the top. She smiled at Dave and
asked how she looked, and he said wonderful. By that
time Resnik had flipped some switches to lower the
room lights and spot the stage. The piano player hit an
arpeggio and the snare drum rolled its command for
attention.

Resnik stepped to the microphone, a slim dark man
with curly hair and long lashes that gave his eyes a
sleepy, hooded look. His smile showed white even
teeth beneath a small neat mustache as he looked out
over the floor, and his white dinner coat was spotless
and unwrinkled. He made a practiced introduction and
then Liza was singing and Dave leaned back, the drow-
siness working on him as he concentrated on the
tune. . . .

In that first instant when Dave Barnum opened his
eyes he had the impression that he had not been asleep
at all; it was only in the next second when full con-
sciousness returned that he knew something was rad-
ically wrong.

It was no one thing. It was a combination of things
that seemed to hit him all at once: the dancing couples,
the orchestra playing, the table in front of him cleaned
of everything but an ash tray, also clean.

Even then he fought for some understanding. He remembered that Liza had just started to sing, that she normally was on stage for twenty or thirty minutes. Only then did he think to glance at his watch, to see that it was 11:35, to understand that he had been asleep for perhaps an hour and a half.

Now, a slow panic taking hold of him, he stared across the room to find the table that Betty and Workman had occupied was empty. He could not locate Liza and he saw his waiter and beckoned, still bewildered and just a little scared. Where, he demanded, was Mr. Gannon.

"Oh, he left," the waiter said indifferently.

"Left?" Dave said, trying not to shout. "How long ago?"

"Quite a while."

"Why didn't you wake me?"

"He told me not to." The waiter slapped an ash from the tablecloth with a flick of his napkin. "He paid the check and said I was to leave you alone. You want anything?"

Dave put down his exasperation and tried to think. He looked over at the corridor leading to the gambling room, then rose, a dark gleam in his eyes and his bony face set. Moving swiftly to the narrow corridor, he brushed past the guard and strode into the inner room.

There were two roulette layouts here, both well attended, the players about evenly divided between men and women. There were two blackjack tables where two dealers, tall and shapely blondes with stony faces and hard bright eyes, were busy with their avid customers. A man named Lacey, who was Resnik's assistant, was watching the roulette tables but Resnik was not present, nor was Gannon. When Dave was sure, he turned and went outside without a word.

The car was gone from its parking place. Sam Resnik's car was also missing from its accustomed spot but Dave did not wonder about it. Instead he approached the attendant and found him no more helpful than the waiter.

"Oh, a long time ago," the attendant said. "An hour, maybe longer."

Dave let it go at that. Understanding that it would take too long to phone for a taxi, he wheeled and broke into a long-legged lope, hearing the attendant call to him but paying no attention as he headed for the motel less than a half mile away.

3

THE NEXT five minutes were interminable, not from the unaccustomed physical effort but from the things that went on inside Dave Barnum's head, the things the doctors had told him, the precautions he had taken when they had first arrived.

"Stay with him!"

That had been the substance of the fundamental warning the doctors had given him. Suicides, they said, were not normal people. Their minds were warped and they could, when opposed, develop a crafty cunning that devoted itself to outwitting those who would thwart them.

"Humor him, but take precautions!"

That was the second tenet of the theory. And he had humored Gannon. He had taken precautions. There were no guns in the bungalow, no sharp instruments. Gannon used an electric razor and he himself had cleaned out the kitchen of all its implements except a bottle opener. The sleeping capsules were kept locked in his bag, and that left only the gas heater, about which he could do nothing except sleep each night with the connecting door open.

The heater had worried him before; it worried him now as he ran through the hot and humid night, feeling the suction of the speeding cars that passed him, the quick breeze that slapped his sweating body.

He tried to forget about the doctors, arguing now that the whole thing was some silly product of his imagination. There was nothing the matter with Gannon. He had shown no suicidal tendencies. Slipping out like that was probably his idea of a joke, his way of getting even for the constant watchfulness on Dave's part.

This was what he told himself but it did little good, so he drove on, mouth open and heart pounding, seeing now the NO VACANCY sign distinctly. Just beyond, and opposite the Coffee Shop, the headlights of a parked car were suddenly switched on, the brilliance of the high beam blinding him momentarily. He was aware that the car angled into the road and as it accelerated past him he automatically noticed that it was a blue Cadillac convertible. Then it was past and he had swerved off the highway, heading for the grassy area between the long, low units.

He saw, vaguely, that there was a light on in Stinson's apartment but the others, those occupied by the transients who would be off in the early morning, were all dark and quiet. Only at the far end were there any other windows alight, and these were in Gannon's half of the bungalow.

He did not think of Betty then, or Workman, but kept on until he could see the outline of the bungalow clearly against the night sky. Suddenly he slowed to a walk, fighting for breath and control of his emotions as he realized there was no car in the adjacent port.

Then why were the lights on?

This was the question he asked himself as he tried to keep a tight hold on his imagination. He found it hard to walk those last few feet to the edge of the building and the lighted window, which was a little closer than the door.

He saw then that the window was closed. The angle of the shutters blocked his vision but he thought he saw a shadow move and he could hear the sound of radio music.

For another moment he stood there incredulously,

knowing Gannon never listened to music. Then the tension hit him and he moved instinctively, away from the window, trying the door and finding it locked, darting then to his own door and stepping through it into the darkened room and the lighted connecting doorway beyond.

Gannon was sitting in the easy chair near the radio, his head back and eyes closed, arms dangling straight down and legs extended, like a man asleep or in a state of collapse. Dave started toward him; then, seeing the wall panel, which had swung outward to reveal the open door of the safe, he felt again the surge of his fears.

"John!" he said, his voice tight. "John!"

Reaching down he shook a limp shoulder, felt the forehead which seemed nearly as warm as his own. He could see no sign of injury, no stain on the clothing. Then, because the thought of suicide remained uppermost in his mind, he remembered the sleeping pills. Still not knowing whether Gannon was breathing or not, he wheeled toward his room and the locked bag where he kept them.

What happened then came without warning. He heard no sound but the radio and the wheeze of his breathing. There was no premonition of danger. He stepped back into darkness, and as he turned toward his bag in the corner something hit him from behind and he went down.

The next few seconds remained forever vague in his memory and what he heard came as from a great distance. He found himself on his hands and knees, conscious but groggy. Through the roaring that filled his head there came to him the sound of someone moving past him, toward the bed. Then the screen door banged.

Somehow he got his head up; then he was on his feet, lurching toward that door as his brain began to clear. Not quite knowing how he did it, he was through and on the ground outside, seeing no one on the lawn and, running now, turning the corner of the building toward the beach as some shadow moved diagonally ahead of him.

It was only an impression. He never really saw the man but he heard a branch crack somewhere ahead and that was enough to keep him going, across the gravel drive to the grassy strip bordering the beach.

Here the light was better. Directly in front of him were sand and small dunes that stretched in humped and odd-shaped abandon toward the white line of surf which broke upon the beach fifty yards away. To the left was an area of undergrowth and palmetto and beach grass, and Dave angled blindly toward it because it offered the only place of concealment.

He heard nothing more than the soft crunch of his shoes in the sand. He saw nothing during those first few steps. The ground itself was in deep shadow and presently his toe caught an unseen root and he went down.

The fall sobered him and made him think. He rose with the sand in his shoes and now he heard someone call from off to the right. When he turned, some movement caught his eye and he retraced his steps, his gaze focusing on the two figures which had started toward him.

He saw then that they were in bathing suits, that one was a girl. In the undergrowth beside him nothing moved and he understood finally the futility of further pursuit. With that he stood where he was, knees trembling and the throbbing growing in his head.

They came toward him, Betty and Workman, still dripping, the girl with a towel and a beach robe on her arm and Workman in trunks, an empty glass in one hand, cigarettes and matches in the other.

Dave said: "Did you see him?"

"Who?" they said.

"I don't know."

"We saw you run in there," Workman said. "At least we thought it was you."

"Someone else," Dave said. "I was chasing him. Or thought I was. He was in the bungalow."

And then he was telling them what he knew and they voiced their reactions, Betty in shocked, awed tones and Workman with blunt incredulity. Somewhere in the distance a car started up and quickly accelerated, and then they were hurrying back to the bungalow, turning on the lights as they entered Dave's doorway and standing finally beside the sprawled figure in the chair.

Workman knelt quickly and reached for a limp hand, lifting it and searching for a pulse beat, concentrating, then glaring in annoyance at the radio. As he did so the music stopped and the announcer said: "This is John Winner, your WTCX platter spinner telling you—"

Dave snapped the machine into silence and now Workman put his ear against John Gannon's chest. When, presently, he straightened, his jaw was lumpy and his gaze was bright and intent.

"He's dead."

Dave heard the words distinctly and they brought no feeling of shock but only incredulity. He looked at Betty and she stared back at him, her young face pale, her gaze stricken.

"But how?" he said.

"Give me a hand."

They stood on either side of John Gannon and took his arms and started to lift him. Then they stopped, staring now at the dark stain well down the middle of the broad back, the darker stain on the cushion.

"All right," Workman's voice was quiet, resigned. "Better leave him as he is." He took a breath, eyes moving to the telephone. "Better call Vantine and get the police. Tell them it's a job for a coroner or medical examiner."

He looked at the girl. He looked down at his own near nakedness.

"We'll get dressed," he said. "I'll be back."

Dave watched them go and then stood where he was, feeling numb and beaten and unable for a while to move at all. Gradually then he became aware of the sand in his shoes, the sweat-stained jacket that clung wetly to his back.

Rousing himself with an effort he slipped off the jacket and dropped it into a chair. Standing first on one leg and then the other, he emptied the sand from his Oxfords and then he went to the kitchen and took a quick swallow from a bottle of Bourbon. When he came back he went directly to the telephone and told the operator to get him the police station in Vantine.

4

CAPTAIN VAUGHN, the acting chief-of-police in Vantine, was a loose-limbed six-footer with a tanned and weathered face and close-cropped dark hair. He wore a wrinkled cotton suit that bulged at each hip, and there was a gold badge on his shirt. Arriving at Seabeach with a motorcycle escort and plenty of assistance, he had asked Dave for a quick fill-in, listened to a partial corroboration from Workman and Betty Nelson, and then sent them into Dave's room to wait. When, a half hour later, he opened the door and asked them into Gannon's quarters, the body had been removed, the seat cushions had been turned, and there was only the open door of the safe to indicate anything had happened.

George Stinson, in his slack suit and sandals, was sitting in one corner, a bewildered look in his bespectacled eyes. A plain-clothes man leaned against the door frame, and two uniformed officers wearing cartridge belts and .45s stood waiting while Vaughn checked the registration cards of the tenants that Stinson had furnished.

"Two of these," he said in his softly cadenced drawl, "have no license numbers, Mr. Stinson."

"Yes." Stinson nodded. "Mr. Tyler and the Lane

couple came by bus. We often get them," he added.
"People who like to travel the roads but don't want to
drive. I understand it's very comfortable."

Vaughn gave the cards to one of the uniformed men.
"Check these," he said. "Don't scare 'em, just find out
if they saw anything tonight. We can't hold all of 'em,
but if you get anybody that's doubtful I'll talk to him.
Maybe I'd better talk to the ones in the bungalows on
each side here anyway."

He walked over to the wall safe. "Kinda clever," he
said. "Who'd know it was here?" He glanced at Stinson,
at Dave and Workman and Betty sitting on the settee.

"We all did," Dave said, "except maybe Betty."

"Oh, I knew," she said quickly.

Workman looked at Dave. "Frank Tyler, too," he said.

Only then did Dave remember the blond man and
the scene that had taken place that afternoon. When
Vaughn said: "Who's Tyler?" Dave told him, giving
what history he knew as well as what had been said
earlier.

Vaughn turned to the other uniformed man. "Get
him," he said. He moved to the table to examine the
things taken from Gannon's pockets: keys, a wallet,
cigarettes, three or four match folders, a handkerchief,
some loose bills and change, a slip of paper which he
unfolded.

"Play the horses much?" he asked of no one in particular.

"Constantly," Dave said.

"Looks like he had a two-horse parlay going. *Trumpter* and *Donnabelle*."

"*Trumpter* won," the plain-clothes man said. "I don't
know about the other."

Vaughn picked up the ring of keys. Stepping over to
the safe he unlocked the inner door. Not bothering to
take anything out, he glanced at Dave.

"I understand Mr. Gannon talked some of suicide.
What can you tell me about that?"

Dave leaned back and took a breath. His head still

throbbed. He felt hot and dirty, discouraged at his own failure, a little sick inside. It took quite a while to tell the story of Gannon's trouble but Vaughn listened without interrupting. Only when it was over did he have a question.

"Who knew Gannon had been talking suicide?"

"Nearly everyone who was around him. Except"— Dave hesitated—"Frank Tyler. He didn't get in until this afternoon."

Vaughn thought it over; then said: "You were acting as a male nurse, but you're not?"

"I'm a lawyer."

"Close friend?"

Dave considered this and replied as honestly as he could. "No, but I owed him plenty. . . . Gannon used to have a small trucking business," he said after a moment. "My father was a bookkeeper for him. When he died I was in my last year at college and Gannon helped me finish because he liked my father. He helped me through Cornell Law School, helped me get a job with this law firm."

He thought of other things as he spoke, of how Gannon, who had not gone to college, had liked to come to Cornell for some of the football games. He would come down to the fraternity house afterward, always in a big car, with his flashy clothes and his tough, hoarse way of talking. Comparing him then with the parents of the other boys had made Dave a little ashamed, and now the shame was on him like a sickness because of those secret thoughts which had been with him long ago.

"This time *he* needed the help," he said, his tone bitter. "I guess I didn't have enough to give him."

Vaughn walked across the room, came back. "Who inherits? And how much?"

"I don't know."

"You're his lawyer."

"I'm with the firm but I didn't represent Gannon."

Vaughn indicated the telephone. "Maybe you could call Boston and find out. It might be important."

Dave looked at his watch and saw that it was after one. He said he would try to get one of the partners at his home, and put in the call. Then, as he sat down again, a new thought came to him.

"Resnik might know about the safe."

"Sam Resnik? How would he?"

Dave told him. He said Resnik had driven up the day before with another man. Gannon had wanted to talk business so he, Dave, had gone into his room.

"And listened some?" Vaughn asked.

"I heard some of it without listening. It was about the Club 80. Gannon had an interest in it and—"

"He what? Since when?"

"I don't know," Dave said. "It was the first I'd heard about it. Later he asked me to draw up an agreement. I batted it out on the typewriter in Mr. Stinson's office, made one carbon."

"What was the substance of it?"

"It was a simple agreement to sell the Club 80 for $120,000."

"To whom?"

Dave said he didn't know. "I left a space for the buyer's name and left the date blank. John said that would do until a detailed agreement could be drawn. After he'd read it he put it in the safe. He asked me if I'd ever had five thousand dollars in my hand and I told him no so he took out this stack of hundred-dollar bills and gave them to me."

"Gave them?" Vaughn scowled.

"Let me hold them," Dave said patiently. "He thought it was funny. He put them back in the safe."

Vaughn went to it and began to empty the contents, piling the various papers on the table beside the things which had come from Gannon's pockets. There were fifteen hundred dollars in new hundred-dollar bills but no package such as Dave had seen.

"These bills were older," he said. "There was a paper band around them, initialed in ink." He hesitated and said: "I think the initials were T.A.K. Maybe a bank teller wrote them."

He watched Vaughn empty the safe, aware finally that both the five thousand and the agreement he had drawn were missing. When Vaughn was sure, he gave Dave a moment's silent regard; finally he shrugged.

"Maybe you know how Resnik fitted in the picture."

"I had an idea John wanted to sell out and Resnik didn't."

Vaughn turned to the plain-clothes man. "Get him, Ed!"

Ed looked doubtful. "Sam's across the county line."

"He'll come," Vaughn said and then, as Ed went out, one of the uniformed officers came in with two men who occupied the bungalows on either side.

One was tall, gaunt, sleepy-eyed, and irritable. He said his name was Weaver and he came from Ashtabula, Ohio. Vaughn explained what had happened and asked if he had heard a shot.

"Yes," Weaver said.

"When?" asked Vaughn with new interest.

"I don't know."

"What do you mean, you don't know."

"Just that, mister. I drove down from Brunswick today. I shook the car half apart over those washboard roads to the border, had a flat, listened to three kids yacking in the back seat all day while the wife told me how to drive. We got here too late for dinner so we had to go to town and when we got back I went to bed."

In his annoyance he managed to get all of this out in one breath and then he said: "I heard something, something that woke me. Could have been a shot, could have been a truck. Short of an earthquake I couldn't be bothered by anything except sleep. I turned over and got some more. I was doing all right until your man came banging on the door."

When further questioning revealed that the man knew nothing more and was interested only in additional sleep, Vaughn dismissed him and turned to the

other man whose name was Bardell and who came from
Plainfield, New Jersey.

Bardell was older, quieter, worried looking, but no
more helpful than Weaver. He was traveling with his
wife, daughter, and son-in-law. They had been to a
movie and stopped on the way back for a drink. He
thought they had returned about eleven thirty and
neither he nor any of his party had been aware of any
shot. At the moment his chief concern was that his wife,
having learned about the murder, would insist on pack-
ing and moving out at once.

Frank Tyler was ushered in a moment later wearing
slacks, a pajama top, and a very sullen look. Vaughn
looked him over carefully, his expression indicating he
did not care much for what he saw. When he was ready
he told Tyler what had happened, reminding him of the
quarrel that afternoon. Finally he looked through the
papers on the table and located the proper agreement.

"The way I get it," he said, "is that after Mr. Gannon
had built the motel he hired Mr. Stinson to run it"—he
glanced at the bespectacled manager—"and made him
a bonus arrangement as an incentive. He assigned Mr.
Stinson one fourth of the *profits*. He assigned his daughter another quarter—this was before she married you—
and a few weeks before your accident, she re-assigned
this interest to you."

"That's right," Tyler said.

"According to this"—Vaughn tapped the agreement—
"all you or Stinson could get while Gannon was alive
was this cut of the profits. Upon his death, or upon sale
of the place, Stinson and Gannon's daughter—which
means you—would get a fourth of the proceeds. You
came here this afternoon hoping you could cash in on
that quarter interest now."

"Well, I thought—"

Vaughn cut him off. "All you were entitled to was a
quarter of the income, and to make sure your share was
cut down, Gannon called the president of the County

Bank & Trust Company at his home and—in your pres-
ence—said he wanted to slap the biggest mortgage
he could get on the place so that when the interest
was paid there wouldn't be so much profit for you to
collect."

He glanced at Dave for confirmation, got a nod, and
then turned to Stinson. "Did Gannon tell you he was
going to mortgage the place?"

"Well—yes."

"When?"

"Before dinner. He—he said he wanted to cut down
Mr. Tyler's share as much as possible, but that he would
make some other arrangement with me."

"Did he tell you the bank might want to go over the
books in the morning?"

"Yes. That's why I was working on them all evening.
So I could get them up to date."

Vaughn grunted softly. "Now it won't matter so
much."

"I beg your pardon?"

"You won't have to worry about the books. Things
are different now."

Stinson blinked. "In what way?"

"The profits aren't going to matter so much. With
Mr. Gannon out of the way you've got a quarter interest
outright. You can sell that interest—if you can get anyone to buy—borrow on it or—"

"I don't believe it."

Vaughn looked round to see who had interrupted. It
was Betty, sitting upright, her chin up and her glance
defiant in a way that made Dave proud of her.

"Mr. Stinson would never do a thing like that."

Vaughn gave her a tolerant glance. "That's your
opinion, ma'am. We're not accusing anyone yet, we're
talking about motive." He turned to give Tyler a long,
silent look, then said: "You got what you came for,
didn't you? What Gannon refused to give you this
afternoon."

"Look here," Tyler said, his tone blustering and his

blond face unpleasant. "If you're insinuating that I had anything to—" The sentence sputtered out in the face of Vaughn's narrowed gaze and then the phone rang to punctuate it.

Vaughn answered, then handed the instrument to Dave. What followed made up a harrowing and unforgettable five minutes. For Mr. Ames, the senior partner, could not understand that John Gannon was dead, not from suicide, but from murder.

"Murder?" he said finally. "Are you sure? You say he was shot? By whom?"

"They don't know yet."

"But how could that happen? You were with him, weren't you?"

"No, sir."

"What's that! But good God, man. That's what you were down there for. Where did it happen? Where the hell were you?"

Dave explained as best he could. He could not bring himself to say he had fallen asleep because it was a nightmarish situation that he could not even understand himself.

"He gave me the slip," he said lamely. "We were at this club and John was playing roulette and somehow he got out without my seeing him. . . . The police want to know if there was a will," he said when he could, "and what the estate amounts to."

"Certainly there was a will," Mr. Ames said. "Drew it up three weeks ago."

Then, as Dave listened to the provisions of that will, his dark-blue eyes widened and his jaw sagged. An odd emptiness gnawed at the pit of his stomach, and though he heard each word distinctly his reaction remained one of utter disbelief. When, finally, he hung up, he swallowed against that awful emptiness and shook his head bewilderedly. He took time to wipe the perspiration from his face and hands, aware that everyone was watching him. When he could he faced Vaughn.

"There was a will," he said woodenly. "I didn't know

about it. He made it three weeks ago. There weren't
any relatives. He left everything to me."

He paused, aware that the room was heavy with heat
and absolutely still. Finally someone sighed. Vaughn's
lips twisted in what might have been a smile. Then,
nothing changing in his voice, he said:

"What's the estate consist of?"

"There was some insurance but he'd borrowed on it.
I don't know about bank accounts but Mr. Ames doesn't
think there was much cash. Aside from that there's the
motel and the Club 80, the building and grounds."

"Building and grounds, hunh? Well, what do you
know." Vaughn rubbed a thumb along the edge of his
jaw and tipped his head. "Speaking of motives," he said
thoughtfully, "you really had one."

Dave did not protest. He did not even feel resentment
at the inference because he knew it was true.

"You come in here and find Mr. Gannon in the chair
and someone slugs you—"

"I've got a lump to prove it too."

"People have slugged themselves before," Vaughn
said mildly. "You'd be surprised how often they try it.
. . . You say you chased someone but you didn't see
him. Neither did anybody else."

"A doctor examined the body, didn't he?" Dave
argued. "He should have some idea when death occurred."

"The doc guessed for me," Vaughn said. "That's about
all I could expect and this shapes up like one of those
cases where a guess isn't enough. Between ten thirty
and twelve is the way he put it."

Vaughn might have had more to say but just then
the screen door opened and Sam Resnik came in with
the plain-clothes man.

If Resnik felt the heat he did not show it. He looked
immaculate in his white dinner coat, his curly hair was
neat, and his pale face was smooth and unworried. He
looked the room over with his hooded eyes and put his
hands in his jacket pockets, thumbs showing.

"Ed tell you?" Vaughn asked. "We've been finding out some things," he added when Resnik nodded. "Like Mr. Gannon owning the Club 80." He hesitated and said: "You and he must have had a deal."

"We did."

Vaughn tapped the papers on the table. "Should be an agreement here."

"Should be," Resnik said. "I can tell you what's in it and save you some time. We were partners. He owned the real estate and I owned the furnishings. I operate. We split down the middle with me guaranteeing a thousand a month rent."

"You got a lease?"

"For three years."

"When does it expire?"

Resnik's glance flicked to the agreement and came back. "The first of the month."

Vaughn nodded, his gaze intent.

"That's next week. Not much time, hunh? And I understand Gannon wanted to sell and you didn't. What's the agreement say about a renewal—or should we look it up?"

Resnik's mouth tightened under the mustache but his tone was level. "It was up to Gannon. He could renew or not. In the event of his death I had the right to keep on at the same figure and for the same term, or take over at a fair appraisal."

"Who was Gannon going to sell to, Sam?"

"Who says he was going to sell to anybody?"

Vaughn nodded at Dave. "He does. He drew up a tentative agreement but left the name blank. So who was here yesterday afternoon talking business?"

Resnik hesitated. For a moment Dave thought he was not going to reply and then he apparently changed his mind.

"Willie Shear."

Somewhere in the room there was a faint, whistling sound and Dave saw that it came from the plain-clothes man. Vaughn's gaze did not waver but his eyes opened and then narrowed in thought. When he spoke he sounded impressed.

"Willie Shear, hunh? Well, Willie's a little out of my territory but I guess he can be questioned too. Until then this could add up to a nice motive, Sam. With Gannon around he could close you out as of next week. With him out of the way you're still in business."

He looked the room over. "Lots of motives," he said. "Nice things to have, but me, I'd rather have the killer and figure out the motive later. Let's get some times," he said, and pulled out a notebook and pencil.

"Mr. Gannon gave you the slip tonight"—he looked at Dave—"because you fell asleep. Or were you drunk?"

Dave accepted the question without resentment because he felt he was responsible for what happened. He did not know why he should fall asleep and could not believe he had. And yet—

"I wasn't drunk," he said. "I must have fallen asleep."

Vaughn consulted his notebook. "Gannon left the club around ten minutes of eleven or so." He looked at Workman and Betty. "Did you see him leave?"

"He came by our table," Workman said. "Said he was playing a trick on Dave. Got a big boot out of it. Said not to wake him. Betty wanted to anyway but I thought she'd better not get mixed up in it."

"When did you leave?"

"A quarter after as a guess."

Vaughn nodded. He asked if it was customary for Betty to swim at night and she said yes, when they were hot like they had been lately. She said Workman had wanted to take a drink to the beach with him but she hadn't wanted any. She was waiting when he came by and knocked on her door.

"When was that?"

"About eleven thirty, I think."

"See anyone you knew?"

"I saw Mr. Tyler. He was walking and we passed him just before we turned in here on the way from the club."

"I was there too," Tyler offered. "At the bar."

"You didn't go swimming right away, did you, Miss Nelson?"

"No. We sat behind a dune and had a cigarette and Carl had his drink. We talked and—"

"For how long? Guess."

"Ten minutes."

"Nearer fifteen, I'd say," Workman said.

"Did you notice anything at all during that time?"

"Yes." The girl frowned, continued hesitantly. "We decided to go in the water and I stood up and took off my robe and I was facing this way when I put it down. That was how I happened to see the car go past."

"Here?" Vaughn asked quickly.

"Along this end of the drive. There's a light outside, you know, and the car was moving slowly and I thought it was going to stop, and then it went on a little farther and I lost sight of it."

"Did you recognize it?"

"I—I think it was Mr. Resnik's. It was the same color and make and—"

Her voice trailed off. Vaughn examined Resnik with new interest but the gambler was looking at the girl, his eyes in shadow and revealing nothing.

"You're mistaken, Miss Nelson."

"It wasn't you, Sam?" Vaughn asked calmly.

"No."

"Can you prove it?"

Resnik's lips twisted. "The way I see it," he said, "you're the one who has to do the proving."

Dave waited, wondering now if Resnik had been the man who had slugged him. He felt sure Betty would not have made the statement if she had not been quite certain about the car, and he expected Vaughn to pursue that line of questioning. Instead, the captain continued as if the information were unimportant.

"The way I figure it," he said, "is that you two"—he glanced at Workman and Betty—"got to the beach around eleven thirty or so. At maybe a quarter of twelve a car went past. You"—he looked at Dave—"got here around ten of."

"About that," Dave said.

"Then it looks as if someone came in here during that half hour with a gun. All but one of you knew Gannon had tried suicide in the past, and you'd think a smart lad who wanted him out of the way would have shot him close up so we'd assume it was suicide—which we probably would have. Except for one thing: the safe."

He paused to look at Dave, continued slowly. "It was open. So if you're telling the truth—and right now I'm not conceding a thing—maybe the killer had the gun in Gannon's back and forced him to work the combination and then Gannon made a break. The gun was in his back and it went off. Maybe only a couple of minutes before you got here. Maybe the killer was looking for the key to the inner safe when you walked in on him."

"Maybe," said Dave. "But it doesn't explain the missing five thousand or the copy of the agreement I typed up."

"No," said Vaughn wearily, "it doesn't. You wouldn't know about that five thousand, would you, Sam?" He looked through his notebook as though expecting no answer, tipped his head. "That gives us a line on everyone but you, Mr. Workman. Where're you from?"

Workman said he was from Santa Monica, California, and mentioned a street and number. Vaughn's brows lifted as he jotted it down.

"Long ways from home, aren't you? What line of business're you in?"

Workman rolled over on one hip so he could get at his wallet. He thumbed through some inner compartments, extracted a card. Vaughn examined it with interest.

"A private investigator, hunh? Just traveling around, or have you got business in this section?"

"Business, I hope."

"Like what?"

"Like looking for a missing heir."

"Who?"

Workman's lips fashioned a thin smile and there were sardonic lights in his amber eyes. "I've been working for ten months on this case. If I find the guy there'll be a bonus. If someone else finds him I'm not so sure about the bonus."

"I have to take your word for this?"

"Write this down," Workman said. "Leeman and Vance," he said, and mentioned a Beverly Hills address and telephone number. "They're the lawyers handling the estate. They can tell you what they want. You could call them."

"I'll do that." Vaughn put his notebook away. "Okay," he said. "That'll do for now. I'll have to ask you all to come down to my office in the morning—I'll let you know when—so I can get your statements. By that time we'll know if the transients saw anything tonight that will help us. . . . If you'll just go over Mr. Gannon's effects and papers with me and sign for them," he said to Dave, "I'll be on my way."

Sam Resnik was the first one out, followed by Tyler and Stinson. Workman and Betty were next, and though she looked back over her shoulder at Dave as she went through the door she did not speak. Not until Vaughn had gone and Dave had turned out the lights. It was when he started to close the door that someone called to him softly from outside. She was standing there alone when he went down the two steps.

"I had to come back." She stood looking up at him, her hand on his arm. "It wasn't your fault," she said. "You mustn't think it was."

She said other things but all he could think of now was that she was worried about him and wanted to comfort him, and he was so strongly moved that he covered her hand with his and drew her close, knowing he had never loved her more.

"Please, Dave," she said. "You mustn't feel too badly."

"All right," he said huskily, wanting to voice so many things he could not seem to say. He pressed her arms and told her he'd be all right, that she must get some sleep, turning her away now and watching until she walked to her room and disappeared inside.

He remembered all this as he started to undress and then, moved by the compulsion of a thought that he had never been able to accept, he knew there was one thing more he had to do that night.

He had removed his shirt and now he replaced it; he put on his tie and jacket. A glance at his watch told him it was twenty minutes after two and when he went outside, the motel was quiet, the windows blackly shining. Automatically turning toward the car-port, he stopped short when he realized the car was gone. For a moment he wondered why he had forgotten to mention the fact to Vaughn and why Vaughn had not thought to ask about it; then he started across the lawn, turning left on the highway and keeping to the side of the road.

5

THE LIGHTS were still on at the Club 80 as Dave had known they would be. There were fewer cars in the parking lot now and as he started across it one of them near the edge looked strangely familiar, so much so that he walked toward it until he could make out the Massachusetts license plate. Then, as he stood there with the bewilderment growing in him, the attendant strolled up behind him.

"How long has that been here?" Dave said.

"Ever since you left."

"Why didn't you tell me then?"

"I tried to," the man said. "You came out and asked about Mr. Gannon and I told you and then, bingo! you were off to the races. I yelled after you but you kept on going."

Dave checked the denial which rose in his throat because when his mind went back he remembered the attendant *had* called after him.

"Okay," he said with all the patience he could muster. "Let's start at the beginning. When I drove in earlier I parked over there." He pointed to a spot near the door. "Right?"

"Right."

"Who moved it?"

"Miss Drake."

"What?"

The attendant took a breath now that it was his turn to be patient.

"I told you Mr. Gannon came out. Miss Drake drove him home. When she came back a few minutes later the spot you had was gone so I had to park it here."

"Oh."

"Yeah," said the attendant in a tone which suggested the matter had been terminated.

The orchestra was playing when Dave entered the club's main room, and there were perhaps a dozen couples dancing, one of them Liza and Sam Resnik. Neither saw him move toward the corner booth he had occupied earlier. They were occupied with themselves and oblivious of their surroundings as befitted people in love, dancing beautifully together, slowly and with an effortless grace.

The waiter who had served Dave before moved up as he sat down. "Back again?" he said disinterestedly.

"For a nightcap," Dave said. "Bourbon and water."

"Yes, sir."

"And bring a flashlight."

The waiter did a take, opened his mouth, then moved off with it still open. When he returned he had the drink and the flashlight. He put them down and stepped back, curiously awaiting the next step in the performance.

"I lost part of a cuff link," Dave said. "I thought it might be here." He took out a ten-dollar bill. "Get me some change, will you?"

When the waiter moved off into the semi-darkness of

the room, Dave slipped to one knee beneath the table, paying no attention to anyone else but spraying the bright beam across the floor. That was when he saw the three tiny capsules under one seat, half-capsules really, blue-and-red-striped containers reminding him of the sleeping capsules he gave nightly to John Gannon but somewhat smaller.

There should, he knew, be a fourth half somewhere around but he did not bother with it now. He snapped off the light and slid back on the seat. The whole operation had taken no more than seconds and he was waiting when the waiter came back with his change.

"Find it?"

"Yes."

"Lucky you."

He took the flashlight and the quarter Dave left and moved off and now Dave sat there, glass in hand, having no feeling of surprise or elation. He only knew that the small, persistent part of his mind that had repeatedly rejected the obvious had been right all the time. . . .

Like the main room, the gambling room at the rear of the Club 80 had lost most of its customers since Dave had been there earlier. One of the roulette wheels had been closed down for the night as had one of the black-jack tables. One of the hard-eyed blondes still dealt watchfully to four die-hard fanatics, and at the roulette table still operating there were about eight players and another eight or ten spectators.

Over by the grilled window in the rear wall, Lacey spoke occasionally to the cashier while he kept an eye on the croupier and stickmen. He was a tall man, nearly bald now, with a pink, close-shaven face and a low-voiced way of speaking. His age defied a precise analysis but was probably somewhere in the fifties, and Dave understood almost at once that Lacey did not yet know what had happened at Seabeach. He was grateful for that because he had some questions in mind, and he began by asking what kind of a night the house had.

"Fair," Lacey said. "For awhile I thought it was going to be too damned good."

"Was Sam here after Gannon left?"

"Hah!" Lacey grinned at the cashier, who grinned back. "I'll say he was here. About eleven o'clock Sam was bleeding plenty."

Dave put on what he thought was an interested look and waited, hoping there would be more. In a moment it came and Lacey seemed to enjoy the telling.

"This guy comes in about a quarter of eleven," he said. "A little, pot-bellied guy with a flashy doll trailing him. He's about half stiff and he pulls out two fifties and gets some five-buck chips. He starts playing the numbers, five at a time, a chip each. He blows fifteen and then the last time he hits on number six, leaves five markers and damned if it doesn't repeat."

He shook his head and sighed, apparently at the memory. "Maybe you don't know it but wheels act different on different nights. Sometimes they hit numbers all over the board and sometimes a certain part of the board seems to get most of the play, like the top third or the middle, or sometimes the lower third. Well, this guy hasn't been watching the wheel. He knows from nothing, but I've been watching and the lower third is getting a lot of the play. Well, he sticks with it, and pretty soon he's playin' the limit and hitting too often. By eleven o'clock—I know because I look at my watch—he's in us for about five big ones and Sam is bleeding all over the floor."

He sighed again. "Then the wheel starts to behave. A couple of zeros and a double-zero and the numbers start getting higher and the chump stays with the lower third. By a quarter after he's dropped his original hundred and he quits. He's had a wonderful time and Sam goes out to take the air—he sure needed it too—and the place quiets down. . . . It could have been rough," he added thoughtfully. "Ten minutes more of that luck and he'd have closed us up. After the way Willie Shear clipped us last week we were a little low on cash."

Dave, who had been listening with only part of his mind, came swiftly to attention, remembering now the effect the name had had during Vaughn's investigation.

"Willie Shear?" he said.

"For twenty-two big ones."

"Twenty-two thousand?" Dave's eyes grew dark with thought. He did not know why any of this should be important but some instinctive impulse told him that it was. "How?" he asked. "I thought there was a house limit."

"There is for the ordinary customer. Willie had a run of luck and he was in us for eleven G's. Then he wants one more spin, red or black. Now the house limit is there to protect the house against a crazy run of luck. A player knows that and he can cash in and blow, or play our way. But Willie's different."

He hesitated, intent on some bit of play at the nearby wheel; then he said: "Willie says let's play for the eleven and if Sam says no the word gets out Sam's a tinhorn. So Sam gets the cash and we spin the wheel and it comes up red, right where Willie is . . . Ah, here's the boss now."

Resnik was moving round the table, headed Dave's way, his gambler's eyes busy. A quick glance took care of Lacey and then he gave his attention to Dave, taking his time, examining the glass in Dave's hand, the knot in his tie before looking him in the eye.

"Have trouble sleeping?" he asked softly.

"I came back to get the car," Dave said. "Liza drove John home and brought it back. I didn't know about it then." He was watching the wheel now and suddenly, moved by some unaccountable impulse, he stepped over, took out a five-dollar bill, and dropped it on number six.

The croupier, without even glancing up, picked up the bill, replaced it with a chip, and stuffed the bill in the table slot. The ball jumped, clicked, came to rest on six. Dave put his glass down, picked up the chips and took them over to the cashier's window. He stuffed the new bills in his pocket and moved back to Resnik, who had watched the operation without changing his expression. Now he chuckled.

"You make it faster than I do," he said. "And you know enough to quit."

"I wanted to see if my luck had changed."

"What else do you want?" Resnik was watching the play again and when Dave made no reply he said: "You didn't come back here for a drink. I'm not so sure about the car; I didn't know about that."

"I thought I might get an answer to a question."

"I'm listening."

"Who's Willie Shear?"

If the name had any effect on Sam Resnik he gave no sign of it. He continued to watch the play with silent interest until Dave thought there was to be no answer. Then he spoke.

"Willie?" he said. "Oh, he's one of the boys."

"Like you?"

"Not exactly."

Resnik waited while another ten seconds ticked past.

"Willie operates on a little larger scale. He's got a place south of Palm Beach that would make two of these rooms. I've heard he's got a big piece of a room outside New Orleans and he's got other interests in Nevada."

He waited again before he spoke.

"Willie's a little hard to pin down. He's got a lot of fingers in the pie."

"And he wanted to buy this place from John."

This time Resnik looked at him, his small neat mustache curving and his eyes opaque and fathomless.

"You could ask Willie about that," he said. "Willie ought to know."

6

CAPTAIN VAUGHN sent a police car for Dave Barnum at eleven the next morning. He was taken to a
small, ground-floor room in the county building to give
his statement to a stenographer, and while he was
waiting for it to be typed, he was escorted into the
captain's office, an airy, corner room overlooking the
street.

Vaughn welcomed him in his slow-spoken way and
waved Dave toward a vacant chair. He was in his shirt-
sleeves, the collar open at the throat and the gold badge
putting a sag in the fabric at one side. He seemed in no
hurry to talk and neither was Dave, so he sat there,
watching the other's dark, weathered face as he examined the cartridge shell in his fingers.

"Found it last night at your place," he said finally.
"That makes it an automatic, probably a foreign one."

"You didn't find the gun?"

"We won't. The ocean's too close."

Vaughn tossed the shell beside the sheaf of papers
that had been neatly piled on the roll-top desk. He
clasped his hands behind his head and leaned back to
observe the street outside. That gave Dave a chance to
consider the choice he had made when he failed to mention the empty capsules in his statement.

He had done a lot of thinking since he had wakened,
most of it tinged with resentment. He had relived in
detail the night before, remembering the shock of finding John Gannon's lifeless body, the humiliation of his
talk with Mr. Ames when he could not explain how
Gannon had managed to be alone. But what moved him
most, what hurt so deeply, was the will that named him
beneficiary and executor.

It made him think of John Gannon in quite a differ-

ent way and told him things he had never suspected.
Recalling the secret feeling of shame he had felt when
Gannon had called on him at college, remembering the
tolerance with which he accepted this last association,
and the superiority with which he had come to view it,
he felt small and petty and horribly ashamed.

Now John Gannon was dead and someone had gone
to considerable trouble to make sure that he, Dave Barnum, was safely out of the way. It did not follow that
the person who had drugged him was the killer, or even
a conscious party to the crime but now, sitting there
with all that resentment working on him, it seemed important that he do what he could to find out who was
responsible.

These were the emotional reasons which prompted
him to withhold his discovery until he had a chance to
follow along on his own, if only for a few more hours.
That there was another and more practical reason for
pursuing this course had become immediately apparent.
For his lawyer's mind had told him that by taking the
empty capsules from the Club 80 he had largely de-
stroyed their value as evidence. There was only his
word to say where he had found them, which was
worthless in itself since he himself was involved. Without corroboration he still could not prove that any drug
had been administered.

He stirred in his chair, his eyes morose and brooding
like his thoughts. The movement caught Vaughn's attention and when he turned he was ready to talk.

"I've been doing some checking."

"On Tyler and Workman?"

"On you, too, friend." Vaughn ran his tongue inside
his cheek, his eyelids drooping. "Your office says you
didn't know about the will."

Dave grinned crookedly. "Does that take me off the
hook?"

"Not quite. Because there's always a chance that you
did know about that will and the office only *thinks* you

didn't. I guess you forgot to tell me about the argument
you two had in the Coffee Shop last night at dinner."

The statement made Dave blink because until this
moment he had forgotten all about it. He shook his
head. He said there hadn't been any argument. He said
he and Gannon had been getting on each other's nerves
the past couple of days and since Gannon was paying
the bills he had a right to sound off if he wanted to.

"The way I get it," Vaughn said mildly, "is that Gannon said he was going to call your office this morning
and have someone else sent down."

"He could have," Dave said, remembering the mental
cotton he had tried to stuff in his ears at the time.

"There was something about changing his will too,"
Vaughn said. "About having someone down to draw it
up."

Dave remembered that too but it shocked him now
to hear it put into words by a man who might be sus-
pecting him of murder.

"But I didn't know I'd been named in that will," he
protested.

"That's what you say. That's what your office seems to
think." Vaughn shrugged and his voice held the same
even cadence. "But I have to consider the other possibility. As things stand you'll own the club and half of the
motel. I don't know how much that would run to after
taxes but it might be between one and two hundred
thousand dollars. That's a lot of money. Two days from
now, if Gannon had lived and changed the will, you
might have had nothing. That's a motive the way I see
it and I'm just telling you why you're not off the hook."

He reached for one of the papers on his desk and
went on as if there had been no interruption.

"Tyler is an actor. I guess you knew that. From what
I get up to now he's got no record except some minor
things—traffic violations, a disorderly conduct charge.
Owes plenty of people and must've needed cash or he
wouldn't have had the nerve to come here and try to

tap Mr. Gannon. Just what in particular he wants the
money for I haven't found out yet."

He put the sheet down and picked up another.
"Workman seems okay. I haven't been able to get in
touch with the lawyers he claims he's working for on
this missing heir job"—he glanced at his watch—"but I
should be getting through to them some time after
twelve, our time. His record up to when he went in
business for himself is all right. A cop on the Santa
Monica force for four years. They say he's smart, ambitious, plenty tough when he had to be. Shot up a
couple of kids in a stolen car mixup. Caused a bit of a
stink but no formal charges." He hesitated and said:
"Would you say that Gannon and Workman had ever
met before?"

Dave thought it over and shook his head.

"What makes you think so?"

"From the things that were said. I was there when
they met. Workman went fishing with us four different
days. I'm sure Gannon never even saw him before."

"Then," said Vaughn, "the only way Workman could
be figured, at least on the face of it, is that someone
hired him to do the job. . . . I've got a timetable," he
said, and picked up some additional sheets.

"I talked to the parking lot man at the club. He says
Liza Drake drove Gannon home, dropped him off, and
brought the car back." He glanced up. "But you didn't
know that. You came back for it after we'd left."

"I didn't know where else it could be," Dave said.

"And I forgot to ask, which may have been a mistake. . . . Also," Vaughn said, "when you came back
for the car you went into the club and had a drink and
spent a few minutes in the back room."

Dave nodded, aware that the Vantine Police Department had been busy that morning and his respect for
Vaughn mounting.

"Tyler, Workman, and Miss Nelson," the captain continued, "arrived about the same time. Tyler had a motive and he had plenty of time to do the job. We haven't

got a motive for Workman yet but he had the time if he worked it right. There was five minutes at least when Miss Nelson was changing for the beach, probably more. She didn't see him until he came to pick her up and I'd be willing to bet he could change faster than she could. It would only take a couple of minutes to go over to the bungalow and do the job."

"Stinson was around all of the time," Dave said.

"I've been thinking about Mr. Stinson. Gannon was going to mortgage the place to cut down the profits. Stinson says Gannon was going to make another arrangement so Stinson could still cash in, but that's only what Stinson says. Maybe Gannon had a different idea. And those books Stinson had to get in order. Who's going to know now whether there was a shortage or not?"

Vaughn expected no answer and when he lapsed into silence Dave said: "Where was Resnik after eleven fifteen?"

"Hah! Out for the air. Riding around."

"Who says so besides him?"

"Miss Drake."

"Oh?"

"Yeah. Says she was with him."

"She's in love with him. She'd say what she had to say."

"Sure." Vaughn nodded. "Miss Nelson's testimony would put him on the spot but maybe Liza Drake could take him off. I don't know. Sam's been in and out of a lot of things. If he did the job it's going to be hard to prove with what we've got up to now."

"So how do you stand?"

"Not so good." Vaughn ran his fingers through his dark, close-cropped hair. "We're going to keep punching but the way it looks now we may have to play this thing by ear . . ."

It was five minutes of twelve when Dave got back to his place and he immediately shucked off his jacket and

opened a can of beer. Then, because John Gannon's
radio habits had become his own, he turned on the
radio to get the noon news, checking as he did so to
see that it was tuned to the right station. He had no
more than settled himself when Betty knocked on the
door.

She wore one of the blue, white-trimmed dresses she
used when working, and the sun burnished brightly the
light-brown hair with its weather-bleached edges as she
stood on the top step.

"Mrs. Craft wants to see you," she said. "She wouldn't
tell me why and she wouldn't come here alone. I said
I'd speak to you."

"All right."

"Now?" she asked. "I have to get back in a minute or
two but if we could go now—"

Dave snatched up his jacket and started across the
lawn with Betty, not knowing just what to expect but
not looking forward to the interview. For Mrs. Craft
was small and neat and sixtyish and, in Dave's opinion,
a gossip. She had been at the Seabeach ten days and
had wheedled from George Stinson a ten per cent re-
duction in rent on a weekly basis. She spent a great deal
of time on the beach under her special umbrella—provided by the motel but claimed by her—knitting and
doing crossword puzzles.

Dave had maintained, not maliciously but mostly to
tease Betty, that Mrs. Craft had never been known to
pass a window without trying to peek in and that, in
addition, she was a secret drinker. Betty, who insisted
on thinking the best of everyone—which was one of the
reasons Dave loved her—defended Mrs. Craft by saying
that if she seemed unduly curious it was simply because
she was lonely.

Now Mrs. Craft opened her door as they approached,
smiling brightly behind her pince-nez and nodding
them into the room. She wore a plain blue dress much
too long to be fashionable and her blue-tinted gray hair
was curled and secured by a net.

"I told Betty," she said when they were seated, "that I thought I should speak to you because you were a personal friend of Mr. Gannon's. That's true, isn't it?"

Dave agreed.

"He was a gambler, wasn't he?"

"Well, at one time he was."

"Yes. And he owned that gambling place down the road."

Dave fidgeted uncomfortably. "He happened to own the property—"

"It's the same thing. I saw that—that woman bring him home last night, a man of his age."

"What woman, Mrs. Craft?"

Mrs. Craft had trouble from time to time with her upper plate. Now she pushed it into place with her upper lip before she spoke.

"I understand she sings at Mr. Gannon's place." She twitched her thin shoulders. "I do not like to speak ill of the dead, especially if he was a friend of yours, but I'm afraid Mr. Gannon was not a good man. Not a good Christian."

Dave felt the irritation rising in him but when he looked at Betty something in her eyes seemed to be asking him for tolerance.

"Mr. Gannon had suffered a great personal tragedy, Mrs. Craft."

This sobered her for a moment and she lowered her glance.

"His daughter, you mean? Yes, I heard about that. A terrible thing for any father, a tragic thing."

She put her shoulders back. She arranged her hands in her lap. "I did not mean to inject my personal feelings into the discussion, Mr. Barnum," she said. "They are not important. The Sixth Commandment says, 'Thou Shall Not Kill.' The guilty must be punished."

She took a breath and leaned forward in a conspiratorial attitude. She waited for their attention.

"Now you understand," she said in a loud whisper, "I do not think Mr. Stinson had anything to do with this awful thing. I like Mr. Stinson. He's a bright young man, polite and obliging and much too overworked, I'm sure. I just thought I should tell you that I saw him going into Mr. Gannon's bungalow last night."

Somehow Dave was not ready for the disclosure and the words jolted him, not so much their message but the manner of delivery. A tightness began to work upon the angles of his bony face and his dark-blue eyes grew cold.

"What time was that, Mrs. Craft?"

"Just after eleven. I know because I had turned my radio off—I always do that promptly at eleven so as not to disturb the other tenants—and I was already undre— I mean I was ready for bed. And I was adjusting the shades and I just happened to see Mr. Stinson."

"You watched him enter the bungalow?"

"Not at all," she said stiffly. "I do not snoop, Mr. Barnum, nor pry into the affairs of others."

Oh, no, thought Dave.

"I detest people who do. I merely happened to see Mr. Stinson walking *toward* the bungalow."

"How far away from the door was he?"

"Why—perhaps two or three steps."

"Then you didn't actually see—"

She interrupted him with a shake of her head. She let him know by the set of her mouth that she was indignant and highly displeased with him.

"I was not spying on Mr. Stinson. I assumed that he went to the bungalow because, walking as he was, there was nowhere else for him to go."

She said other things that Dave did not hear because he had drawn his own conclusion. Stinson had been walking toward the bungalow and Mrs. Craft had not actually seen him enter, not because she hadn't continued to look, but because the angle of the building had cut off her view.

"I thought I should tell you first," she said, rising and adjusting the skirt of her dress, "because you were a personal friend. Betty has told me you are a lawyer.

You could tell me whether I should go to the police. I've given the matter a great deal of thought but—" She shrugged and let the sentence dangle.

"I'm hardly in a position to advise you, Mrs. Craft," Dave said. Then to shock her a bit, he added: "Because I happen to be under some suspicion myself."

Her little eyes opened wide. She said: "Well!" with a sort of explosive inflection.

"Perhaps you ought to think about it a little longer," he said as he opened the door. "Until you know what you should do."

Betty kept silent until they were approaching the Coffee Shop and then she stopped. "You weren't very nice to her," she said.

"Nice to her?" Dave growled. "Why the—"

She cut him off. She said he mustn't say it, whatever it was. She gave him a small smile but she was standing close now and he could see the disturbed depths of her hazel eyes.

"Do you have to tell Captain Vaughn?" she asked.

"Probably."

"You practically advised her not to tell right away. Why can't you wait?"

Dave started to tell her that the comparison was not a fair one. He still felt responsible for what had happened. He wanted most of all to see the guilty one caught and, if possible, he wanted to feel he had a hand in that eventuality. But he did not know how to explain this to Betty without sounding corny. There was, however, no reason why he had to hurry to Vaughn; there were a couple of things he wanted to do first on his own.

"You can't make yourself think Stinson is guilty," he said, "because you like him."

"It isn't liking exactly. I've known him longer than you and I won't believe it until I have to."

Dave said all right and then, wanting to change the subject, he asked her what her plans were for the afternoon.

"It's my afternoon off," she said. "I'm going to Boothville."

"To see your dear old college pal."

She smiled and nodded. She said it was a hen party.
Dinner and gossip and a movie. . . .

Captain Vaughn appeared after lunch. He spent some
time in Stinson's quarters and then went over to see
Workman. When he stopped by the bungalow he gave
no indication of what he had come for but he did offer
one bit of information.

"Workman was on the level on that missing heir
case," he said. "I talked with the lawyers handling the
estate. Guy named Albert L. Colby. He hired Workman
originally and when he died six months ago the lawyers
kept him on. Only it ain't a man he's looking for but
Colby's daughter. Name's Elise and, like Workman said,
he gets five thousand out of it if he locates her. That's
all they'd tell me over the phone."

7

STANDING WELL back of the Club 80 was a two-
story frame building which housed storerooms and
garages on the ground floor, and rooms for some of the
help above. A railed stairway led to a gallery from
which the rooms opened, and shortly after two o'clock
Dave Barnum went along this to the door at the end.

He knocked twice, peering through the screen, and
when there was no answer he pushed into an airy,
squarish room that was unmistakably feminine in character and not particularly neat. The ash trays had not
been emptied recently; there were some dirty glasses
on one window sill. The studio couch, which apparently
doubled as a bed, had been made. Three decorative
pillows had been fluffed out and propped along the
wall, but articles of clothing and underclothing clut-

tered the spread, indicating that the owner might be
at the beach, which was what he had hoped.

A closed door, apparently leading to a closet, stood
on the left, and after his first glance about he strolled
toward the only other door, which was open and opposite the first. This led to a dressing room where there
was a vanity and mirror and some built-in chests.

To Dave's masculine eyes the vanity was a mess, the
odor arising therefrom only slightly less than overpow-
ering. Powder was strewn all over the top, and the seat
and floor nearby were flecked with it. There were bottles and jars and vials and boxes of tissue, greases and
ointments and lotions. There were two drawers and
these held other vials as well as certain beauty aids and
instruments necessary to the well-groomed nightclub
chanteuse.

The whole procedure was a little embarrassing somehow, but Dave stayed with it until he had examined
each object; only then did he go into the adjacent bathroom where he stepped immediately to the medicine
cabinet.

Here, in back of the mirror, were, in addition to the
usual toilet essentials, a dozen or more bottles, and he
read the prescriptions on five of them before he found
one that interested him, a small, round container of
green glass, the label of which read: *As required. For
aid to sleeping.*

Unscrewing the cap, he removed the cotton and then
tipped a capsule into his palm. When he saw its color
he grunted softly, replacing cotton and cap while a
slow excitement began to build inside him.

Back in the other room where the light was better, he
started to examine the capsule more closely. Then, suddenly, his head came up and his mouth tightened. As he
listened he heard the unmistakable sound of footsteps
on the outside stairs; when those steps started along the
gallery he acted on impulse, opening now the one
closed door which he had left untouched and stepping
blindly into a closet that was hot, stuffy, and perfumed.

Seconds later the screen door banged and Liza Drake came in.

With his eye to the crack he had left open, but having none of the feeling of a Peeping Tom, he saw her toss her robe and beach bag on the couch. She reached behind her to unsnap her halter, shrugging out of it and flipping it on top of the robe. She stretched once, her arms high, half turning as she did so. That gave him a momentary glimpse of a smooth, two-toned torso that was magnificently molded and presented in profile.

Then she was gone. When he heard the shower start, he tiptoed to the door and eased himself out.

At the foot of the stairs, he lit a cigarette, discovering as he did so that he was perspiring freely. Only then did he experience any sense of guilt and now, as he glanced round, he saw a jumper-clad man watching him from the garage doorway at one side.

Dave pretended the man did not exist. He adopted what he thought was a nonchalant air. He smoked his cigarette with studied slowness and when he thought five minutes had elapsed he went back upstairs and banged on Liza's door. When she opened it a moment later she was wearing a pale-blue robe. Her black hair, which she usually wore pulled straight back to a low-lying bun, was wet at the ends and pinned high. She was massaging her nape vigorously with a wadded towel.

Her dark eyes said she was surprised to see him but her voice was pleasant enough.

"Hi," she said. "Come in."

He stepped past her and when she came up to him he gave her a long unsmiling look that did not seem to register. She pushed a chair around and gathered her things from the couch, stopping to straighten the spread before she moved into the dressing room to get rid of the things in her hands.

When she came back she tightened her robe and apologized for the mess, emptying ash trays now and still not looking at him. She said she had not expected

callers. He let her go on, saying nothing until she ran
out of breath. Then he asked if she had heard about
Gannon.

She sat down suddenly on the couch. She said yes.
She said it was terrible, she was shocked, she couldn't
believe it. When she ran out of words he took the capsules from his pocket and arranged them neatly on the
tabouret before her, the full one, the three halves. Finally he looked at her again, giving her the silent treat-
ment and seeing a new stiffness take possession of her
face.

"I was here before," he said. "I looked around. I
found the capsules in the medicine cabinet." He explained where and when he had found the halves.

"It wasn't the waiter," he said. "He would have
spiked my drink before he came to the table. That
leaves you and John Gannon and Resnik."

She wet her lips. She stuck her chin out, a very de-
termined chin. Her dark eyes returned his stare and her
voice was bold and indignant.

"Wait a minute! Are you trying to tell me I gave you
a Mickey?"

"Somebody did."

"Who says so besides you?"

That stopped him because he had not expected such
defiance. He tried again, patiently.

"I didn't make it up," he said. "I didn't fall asleep."
He touched the capsules with the tip of his finger.
"They're the same, aren't they?"

"They're the same color, if that's what you mean."

He studied her a moment, no longer quite so sure but
thinking too that she was more on the defensive than
was necessary.

"Maybe it was just coincidence."

"I wouldn't know. I'll bet you can get capsules like
that in any drugstore. It's what's in them that counts."

"You don't know anything about them?"

"Not a thing."

"You thought I'd fallen asleep."

She folded her arms across her breasts, tightening the fabric. "I don't like this third-degree routine," she said, and this was not the voice of the girl he had talked with during the past week; this was another who had had to fight with life for what she wanted.

"I don't like what happened to me last night," he said evenly. "I don't like what happened to John Gannon. I'm going to do what I can to find out *why* it happened. If you don't want to talk to me let's call Vaughn. Let's get him over here."

She thought that one over, the determination still there in her mouth and jaw but a disturbance growing now in the depths of her eyes. She went back to his earlier remark, no longer quite so hostile.

"Certainly I thought you were asleep. So did Mr. Gannon."

"Who told him?"

"Why—I don't know. I'd finished my number and went into the gambling room a minute, and somebody—it might have been Carl Workman, or maybe it was Sam —told him. I went out with him and looked at you."

She swallowed and said: "He got a kick out of it. He said you'd been getting too cocky and maybe this would teach you a lesson. He paid the check and told the waiter to be sure he didn't wake you. I asked him what he was going to do and he said he was going home. I told him I'd drive him if he liked and bring the car back so you'd have it to get back in. So"—she dropped her hands, palms open—"that's what we did."

She said other things, most of them repetitious, and as he watched her it occurred to him that he had gone about as far as he could without some help. Then, his thoughts moving on, he said:

"Have you talked much to Carl Workman?"

She blinked at his digression. "Some. He's down here almost every night."

"Has he asked a lot of questions?"

She laughed shortly but without bitterness.

"Most men do," she said with some evasiveness.

"Like what?"

"Oh—like where you're from, and who you know, and how did you get started, and what are your plans." She laughed again. "I've answered a million questions, a lot of them propositions that were monotonous but hardly flattering."

"And where *are* you from? Originally, I mean."

"California. A place called Southgate."

Dave gave her a small smile and said California seemed to be pretty well represented in that particular neighborhood.

"You," he said, "and Workman. Resnik was out there too, wasn't he?"

"For a while. I didn't know him then though."

"Frank Tyler, too. He was here last night. Know him?"

This time he got a reaction but he did not know what to make of it. For now her glance evaded him and she leaned over to open the cigarette box on the tabouret. It was empty and she straightened, the V gaping in her robe though she did not seem to notice it.

"Tyler," she said, accepting the cigarette he offered. "No, I don't think so."

"Southgate," he said when he had given her a light.

"Not far from L.A."

"Any family?"

"Not really."

"What do you mean, not really? What about your father?"

"I don't remember much about him. He ran out when I was little. A bum, according to my mother." Her glance slid past him and distance grew in her eyes. "Not that she was much better," she added.

"She got work as a waitress. I had to take care of myself mostly. She was away most of the day, and some nights she didn't come home at all. By the time I was fifteen I'd had all I could take. I was well developed for my age, with plenty of everything, and I looked older. It was easy to lie about my age so I got a job as a waitress too."

Still not looking at him she said: "Wherever there was a band I pestered the boys and the boss for a chance to sing, even if it was only a three-piece combination that could hardly stay with the beat. At first it was mostly for nickels and dimes but I kept at it. Because I knew what I wanted and I knew if I tried hard I'd get it."

Watching her as she said these things, Dave somehow thought he understood what she meant. He took a guess.

"Sam Resnik?"

She smiled then. It was a nice smile, and for Liza an almost shy smile that barely showed her fine white teeth.

"A man," she said by way of correction. "It turned out to be Sam but all the time I had someone in mind just like him. I couldn't kid myself too long about my standing as a singer, not and stay smart. As a voice I'm worth maybe a hundred a week. My body, properly dressed and exhibited, is always worth another hundred to anyone who can afford to pay. Throw in the experience and know-how in handling the paying customer and it adds up to three or four hundred, maybe five at the most, providing the boss really likes me. But not for long. A few years with luck."

She smiled again. "That's quite a speech," she said. "I wish we had a drink."

Dave said he wished so too, and waited, and now she looked down at the ring on her left hand, turning it half consciously as if to admire it secretly and all it stood for.

"It was worth waiting for," she said, more to herself than to him. "Because I've known all kinds of men, the good and the bad, the heels and the right guys. I've had to know them, had to learn which ones you can flatter, which ones you pamper, and which you have to insult. You learn how to duck, too, but you have to get along

with them, mostly, because it's the men who lead the
bands, and do the booking and run the nightspots.
They're the ones that have the jobs to hand out and all
you have to do is learn how to handle them."

She leaned over to crush out her cigarette, and the
robe gaped again and this time she noticed it and fixed
it, expertly and without embarrassment.

"I like men," she said, "most of them. Somehow I
don't think my father was the bum my mother tried to
make out. Knowing her better than him I'd lay odds it
was more her fault than his that things didn't work out.
What it takes is the right man and the right woman."

"That's how it is with you and Sam."

She nodded, peeking at the ring again, and now, as
she fell silent, Dave thought he could begin to understand the sort of woman she was.

The determination was there in the chin and the full
mouth, the straight, strong brows, for without determination and a certain singleness of purpose she could
never have lasted this long. But there was more to it
than that. For it seemed to him now that the right man
could call forth much warmth from this woman, a great
intensity of feeling. But there would be possessiveness
too, and jealousy on occasion. Above all there would be
an unwavering loyalty that would endure so long as
that love lasted.

She had settled for Sam Resnik and, remembering
the things Vaughn had said, he knew that Liza would
continue to swear that she had been with Resnik the
night before, after he had left the club. Nothing except
some perfidy on his part would ever change her story.

And so he rose, knowing he had done all he could
here, not sure how much of what he had heard was the
truth but recognizing, too, an undertone of sincerity in
many of the things she had said. His movement served
to break the spell she had so recently woven about herself, and the softness left her dark gaze when she rose
and asked what he intended to do about the capsules.
Once again she was on the defensive, and he saw this

and told her he did not know. He said he would let her know.

8

BY THE time Dave Barnum returned to the bungalow he had made up his mind about the capsules. His own experiment had proved nothing actually. He had satisfied his own curiosity to some extent but that, he realized now, was unimportant. His job was to help Captain Vaughn in any way he could, regardless of who happened to get hurt in the process. He had withheld this information too long as it was, and now it was up to him to admit it and take the consequences.

He put in his call to the Vantine police station at once, and when, presently, Vaughn came on, he said he had a confession to make.

"Good," Vaughn said. "I was beginning to think we weren't going to crack this one. I'll send a stenographer right over."

"It's not that kind of confession."

"Oh," Vaughn said in a tone that suggested he had known it all the time but had played it straight. "You had me worried."

"I'll bet," Dave said and then he was telling what he knew, starting at the beginning and trying to explain as best he could his own personal reasons for wanting to have a hand in exposing the one who had tricked him.

He fully expected an explosion of some kind when he finished but it never came. There was a moment of silence and when Vaughn finally answered his tone was resigned and only mildly disgusted.

"It's too bad," he said. "What some of you amateurs can do to louse up us pros is enough to break a guy's heart."

"I should have told you this morning."

"No," Vaughn said, thereby demonstrating again his ability to think quickly and with precision, "you should have told me about your hunch last night before you even went back to the club and you ought to be lawyer enough to know why."

"I think I do—now," Dave said, remembering his own reasoning on the matter when he had made his statement that morning.

"Now is no good. Last night we could have gone along with you. *We* would have found those half capsules. We would have photographed them, labeled them, and put them under lock and key as evidence. We could have checked immediately and we'd know by now if they came from Liza Drake's bottle."

He grunted softly, an unflattering sound. "*You* say you found them under the table but that's no good because you yourself are involved. For all you can prove, it could still be a plant of yours. If those capsules came from the Drake woman's bottle, whether she knew it or whether she didn't, that bottle will be deep in the swamp by the time I get out there—unless she's a lot dumber than I think she is. . . . God damn it, Barnum!" he said, still more disgusted than angry. "Why couldn't you have played that one smart?"

Dave had no answer. He felt about six years old. He mumbled something about being sorry and after another moment of strained silence he heard Vaughn sigh.

"Okay," the captain said. "We'll go out and see her. Maybe she'll scare. Maybe something'll come of it but I'll lay you eight to one it'll be too late to do us much good. You can hang on to those capsules, just in case."

The connection was broken to punctuate the sentence, and Dave hung up. The moment he did so, someone knocked at the door. He had heard nothing prior to that but when he opened it George Stinson smiled apologetically and asked if Dave could spare a minute. He wore tropical-weight slacks and a loud, loose-hanging shirt this time, but the same open-work sandals. He adjusted his glasses as he sat down and he coughed behind his hand, coloring slightly as he cleared his throat, as though embarrassed at what he had to say.

"I thought I should ask what you intend to do and if you have any plans yet," he said in his mild-mannered way.

"About what?"

"Why"—Stinson waved his hand—"about the motel."

Dave told him the truth. He said to be perfectly frank he had not even thought about the motel. Stinson nodded. He said he could appreciate that. He rubbed his palms together and then placed them on the chair arms. He let his glance stray to the window and the grounds outside and it was obvious now that he had some things on his mind which he wished to discuss. Presently his glance came back and he cleared his throat.

"Did Mr. Gannon ever say anything to you about selling the motel?" he asked.

"No. Did he to you?"

"Yes, the first day he arrived."

He hesitated to see if Dave had any comment to make and then, unexpectedly, he digressed.

"This is the first job I've ever had as manager," he said. "I was an assistant to the owner of a larger place near St. Augustine when I met Mr. Gannon. He used to stay there regularly and I guess he took a liking to me because when he built this place he offered me the job. He never had any intention of operating it himself but he wanted someone he could depend on who wouldn't be too expensive. I had a hand in furnishing it. I've been here ever since."

Dave nodded. He said by the looks of things Stinson had done an excellent job.

The manager acknowledged the compliment with a small nod of his head and continued his story.

"I was to have two hundred and fifty a month and my quarters, plus a very small percentage the first year, or three fifty and no percentage. Well, I figured there wouldn't be too much profit the first year anyway, so I took the three fifty. Then the second year Mr. Gannon gave me the proposition I now have and, frankly, it has been reasonably profitable for me."

He glanced out of the window again and said: "Of course, I've worked hard. A man has to know quite a bit about a lot of things to run a motel successfully. You have to do some accounting to take care of the tax and employee problems. You get to be an amateur landscape gardener and if you try to run a small restaurant like we do you're in trouble unless you get someone like Betty Nelson to take over. You have to know something about housekeeping, maintenance, purchasing, insurance, plumbing, heating, air conditioning, law, and diplomacy."

He smiled and said: "In spite of all that, I like it. It's what I want to do and, as I say, I've done quite well, but I suppose it's only natural when you like your work to want to be the boss and have a business of your own. I've saved some money, though not nearly enough to consider buying a place; that's why I was—well, rather excited when Mr. Gannon said he had begun to think about selling."

Dave had been listening to everything Stinson said but now he found himself more interested in the man himself than the subject he was discussing. He realized again that Stinson had a very good motive for murder, and yet he found it hard to believe anyone so inoffensive looking could be capable of such violence. The man's coloring, the reddish tinge to his sandy hair and lightly freckled skin, suggested a temper and a disposition that could be highly volatile under the proper provocation. That the temper never seemed to show proved nothing. The pale-blue eyes seemed as mild as his voice but this, Dave realized, could be due to the fact that he knew so little about the man.

This was his first job as top man. He had been on it for something over three years. He looked to be about thirty-five now, though this was but a guess, which meant that at thirty-two he had only progressed as far as the assistant manager of a motel. . . .

With an effort he pulled this thoughts back to the matter at hand. "It would be a pretty expensive proposition for Mr. Gannon, wouldn't it?" he asked.

"I beg your pardon?"

"In case of a sale you were entitled to twenty-five per cent."

"Well—yes."

"He had also assigned the same interest to his daughter. At the time he spoke to you," Dave said, while his mind added the thought: *if he ever spoke to you at all,* "his daughter was dead and he did not know she had re-assigned her interest to Tyler. I don't know the laws of inheritance in California. I don't know what might have happened to the daughter's estate if she hadn't re-assigned her interest. The point is, if Mr. Gannon had lived and sold this place he would have had to pay you—"

"I see what you mean," Stinson said, interrupting. "I meant to mention that. Mr. Gannon said the same thing. He said that when he made the agreement with me he had expected to keep the motel for a great many years and that if I built the business up I would be entitled to twenty-five per cent but now, after only three years— well, he was quite frank about it. He said, and I can quote him, 'I was too damn generous with you, George.'"

"So what did he suggest?"

"He said he wanted at least $180,000 for the place. On that basis I'd be entitled to $45,000 by the terms of the agreement. But he said if I insisted on that amount he simply couldn't afford to sell at all. If I'd agree to make a new deal with him he'd give me a flat $25,000 providing he got his price."

Dave nodded. So did Stinson.

"Naturally," he said, "I jumped at the chance. I said it would be more than fair. Because you see"—and now he leaned forward and a new brightness began to work in his eyes—"I have my eye on this property in Eaton. It's smaller, and run down, and I can buy it for $60,000. I have $15,000 of my own. With Mr. Gannon's $25,000 I'd have $40,000 and I know I could arrange with a bank to buy with no more than $20,000 down, which would leave me that much to put into new furnishings and maybe two more units. The painting and things like that I could do myself."

Yes, Dave thought. *But now you won't have to borrow. You can buy the property outright.*

That thought remained with him because, as with Liza Drake, he could not tell how much of what he had heard was truth and how much was neatly manufactured for his benefit. He realized Stinson had spoken again.

"I'm sorry," he said.

Stinson had leaned back and most of the brightness had gone from his gaze.

"I said, I suppose I'll have to wait."

"For a while, yes," Dave said. "They're mailing a copy of the will down and it will have to be probated—I don't know where yet. I don't know about the tax situation. I'll have the authority to make some small advances but—"

He shrugged and left the sentence unfinished. Stinson sighed and stood up. He said he understood. He did not mean to be hasty. As he backed toward the door he added that he would be glad to co-operate in any way he could.

Frank Tyler came over a few minutes later with a similar idea in mind but in his case there was no hesitancy or finesse in his presentation. What he had in mind was money, and how soon could he get it.

"Let's get that mortgage John was talking about yesterday," he said. "That way I can collect part of my share and be on my way."

Dave looked at him with wonderment and then disgust, the anger rising in him as he examined the blond

features which he had once thought handsome and
seemed now to reflect only impatience, petulance, and
greed. Seeing him lean indolently against the doorway,
all he could think of was that Tyler had caused Gannon
all his trouble, killing his daughter and, for all he knew,
the man himself.

Tyler must have sensed the thoughts behind Dave's
look because he colored slightly. He sat down abruptly
and when he spoke, he spoke not as an actor reading his
lines but bluntly and with aggression.

"Okay," he said. "So I'm the heavy in the piece. I ran
off with Alice Gannon. I took her away from a comfortable home and put her in a cheap two-room apartment. To wrap it up neat I drove the car that killed
her. . . . Did you know her?" he asked abruptly.

"Slightly."

"The greatest kid in the world. I've heard how Gannon cracked, trying to jump and all that. I don't blame
him. He was entitled to plenty of remorse. But what
about me? I loved her and I killed her. You think I'll
forget that? You think it's something you get over?
Ever?"

Dave listened with sudden amazement. He took another good look at Tyler and now he saw ridged jaw
muscles, the stormy brown eyes. His hair was tousled
and he needed a shave and his resentment was undis-
guised. He put his fists on his thighs, arms akimbo.

"I'm an actor," he said. "I guess you don't think much
of actors. Most people don't, especially unsuccessful
actors; but that's what I want, that's what I am. I was
lucky enough to get east last summer. I landed a job
on the Cape and I met Alice and we fell in love. It's as
simple as that. I met Gannon just once and he hated
my guts."

He hesitated, scowling, as though at the unpleasant
thoughts his words had conjured up.

"He said I wasn't good enough for her, and in that he
was right, but he misjudged Alice. She was twenty-four

and she was in love and she wanted to get married. She said her father would get over it once he got used to the idea. She never dreamed that anything else could happen. We wired him from New York and again from Chicago. She wrote him from L.A. and wrote him again, and there was no answer, and after a third letter she began to get the idea. It broke her up because Gannon was the only man she'd ever really known until I came along. He was her father and she loved him and she couldn't understand why he should treat her that way."

He took a breath and said: "She began to drink a little more than she should and who was I to argue with her? I could hardly keep her in coffee and cake. She had to stick around this lousy little flat because I had to have the car so I could keep looking for work. I got some now and then. An extra spot sometimes, a couple of days here and there, once in a while a radio or TV shot but nothing regular. You know why she re-assigned me her rights in this place? I'll tell you," he said.

"Because we were broke and we thought with that interest in my name I might be able to borrow a bit on it. I owed people here and there and I got tired of hitting my friends for ten or twenty bucks. I took the assignment to my agent and he turned out to be a better guy than I suspected. He let me have five hundred and told me to forget the collateral. To celebrate, Alice and I lifted a few. We decided to go out for dinner to this place down the coast. We got in the car and a trailer truck forced me off the road."

He stopped abruptly and his mouth took on a sardonic twist. "Quite a monologue, huuh?"

Dave could think of no reply. The driving sincerity of the hard-spoken words carried a ring of conviction and he guessed that this much, at least, was truth.

"So much for the prologue," Tyler said. He leaned back and crossed his legs. "So how about the mortgage?"

"There won't be any mortgage," Dave said, "until I find out what the tax situation is, and maybe not then."

For another moment, Tyler's gaze remained stormy. Then, unexpectedly, as though deciding bluster would get him nowhere, he grinned.

"I'd be willing to sell out at a discount for cash."

Dave shook his head.

"Then how about an advance?"

"Not from me. Not now anyway."

"I could go to court."

"Why don't you?"

Tyler thought it over, apparently too concerned with his own problems to take offense.

"I'll tell you why I want it," he said. "Why I came here to see Gannon. I didn't think he knew Alice had re-assigned her interest to me and I didn't expect him to pay up. But I was hoping I could make a deal. Look, how much is this place worth?"

Dave told him what Stinson had said.

"That's what I mean. I thought maybe if I offered to give back this interest that I would eventually be collecting on, for say ten or twelve thousand now, why then Gannon might go for it. It would be a good deal for him, wouldn't it?"

He did not wait for an answer but said: "The reason I want that ten is because I've got a hook-up with a smart young producer-director and a writer who's got a sweet idea and knows how to write a sound television script. What we want is to make a pilot film. We have to have that if we're going to peddle the show. We think it's a natural, and this ten with what they've got would put it over."

He stood up and began to pace the floor, his gaze roving. "You heard what happened yesterday. I didn't even get a chance to speak my piece. Gannon blew his stack." He turned to look at Dave. "Now it's different. I've really got a quarter interest in this outfit, haven't I? Do you think a bank would give me a loan?"

Dave rose, knowing that one thing was clear. If Tyler's proposition would wait, he would most certainly be able to raise all the money he needed. But he did

not say so. He did not know why. Something about the
man's personality continued to rub him the wrong way
and he still did not know what he was really like inside.

"Why don't you go to a bank and ask?" he said. "Then
you'll know."

With that, and having had quite enough of Tyler, he
went into the kitchen for a can of beer. He took his time
opening it and when he came back the big man was
gone.

9

BETTY NELSON'S small and ancient coupe was gone
from its accustomed place when Dave drove the Gannon sedan behind her unit. The transients had not yet
started to arrive and the motel had a quiet, deserted
look as he passed the office and turned south into the
swift-moving traffic.

Overhead the sun was bright, and heat rose in steady
waves from the highway, infiltrating the car so that even
the breeze seemed uncomfortably humid. The roadside
stands looked cheap and discouraged with their lack
of customers, and the shirt-sleeved citizens of Vantine
moved slowly and kept to the shady side of the street.

Dave drove straight on through, knowing what he
wanted to do and making his plans even though the idea
persisted that this trip would probably prove to be a
fool's errand. It was really nothing more than a certain
native stubbornness that kept him going until, a half
hour later, he came to the town of Eaton, which proved
to be little more than a crossroads with an overhanging
traffic light, a filling station, a drugstore, a half block of
one-story shops and offices and, up ahead, a movie
theater with more offices on the second floor.

He slowed down after he had passed the traffic light,
keeping well to the side of the road until he saw the

sign of a motel. He turned into the drive before he realized that the buildings were new and attractive, the grounds tastefully landscaped and kept. The sign said *The Plantation* and Dave kept on going until he circled back on the highway and headed back toward Eaton, knowing full well the sixty thousand dollars George Stinson had mentioned would hardly be more than a modest down payment on such an establishment.

Back in the village he turned right, toward the ocean, and parked in the nearest space. When he stepped to the sidewalk he found himself in front of a small, square, stucco building. Over the door a sign said: *George Bradbery—Real Estate.* Underneath, in smaller lettering, were the words, *Sales, Leases, Rentals . . . Business, Residential . . . Notary Public.* The two windows each held a bulletin board on which were listed current offerings. Beside the boards were glossy prints of some of the more outstanding bargains.

Dave opened the screen door and went inside. Immediately in front of him were three yellow-oak chairs and a wicker table on which were some real estate magazines. Beyond this and facing the street was a large flat-top desk and still farther back a girl nearly surrounded by filing cabinets was pecking at a typewriter.

George Bradbery was a plump, perspiring man clad in poplin trousers, supported by suspenders, and a short-sleeved sport shirt. He had a large blueprint of some development spread out before him and when he glanced up and saw Dave he rose immediately and came forward, his smile genial, his manner hearty. He offered a warm, damp hand when Dave introduced himself. He said:

"Mr. Barnum, I'm real pleased to meet you. Sit down." He leaned back, the chair springs protesting with the strain. "Now, sir, what can I do for you?"

Dave smiled back and it was a real nice smile when he worked at it; his manner was as pleasant as Bradbery's. He said he was going to be perfectly frank. He had no intention of doing business today. He just wanted to make some inquiries and look around; if Mr. Bradbery was too busy he could come back another time.

"Never too busy, Mr. Barnum. If a man came in here cold, like you, and offered to buy a piece of property without looking around I'd think there was something wrong. Look around. Yes, sir, that's the way to operate. Where're you from, Mr. Barnum?"

"Massachusetts."

"The Cradle of Liberty. And if you've got the idea like some people from the North that the 'Crackers' are out to swindle you, you can rest your mind while you're in my hands. I'm from Pennsylvania myself. Came down here five years ago and it was the smartest thing I ever did. Frankly, Mr. Barnum, I'm a one-hundred-per-cent booster for the town of Eaton, and I'll tell you why."

He uncradled his fat neck and began to rock in his chair. "Because it's got everything. Climate—the Gulf Stream comes in pretty close here, which means we're warmed in the winter and cooled in the summer—safe bathing, a wonderful beach. There's an inlet from the sea a mile down the road and that means we've got some of the finest fishing in the whole United States. You'll see the day when this town'll be built up solid for miles around. Can't help it. Where're people going to go? Look what happened to Lauderdale, Hollywood. Look what's happening to Delray."

Dave felt himself nodding agreement with each statement. He kept his grin under control. It wasn't necessary to say a word. All he had to do was nod. He watched Bradbery wave a dimpled hand to the westward.

"Inland across the railroad tracks," he said, "you'll find the highest spot in this whole county. Eaton Heights. You couldn't call it a hill. You couldn't hardly call it much of a grade, but it's there just the same. You can see the ocean, you get a breeze. Today you can buy a sixty-foot lot for as little as eight hundred and fifty dollars. Tomorrow"—he tipped one hand—"who knows.

Houses going up right and left. Retired people, a lot of them. People that want to be near the ocean but not too close, people that want value."

He belched and said: "Pardon me. . . . Down here, of course, we're zoned for business. We're not going to blow up into any overnight boom, you understand. Just steady, solid growth to accommodate the people who come here to live. Building going on all around you. All you have to do is use your eyes. A hundred and fifty yards down this road you'll come to the Inland Water-way—Intra-Coastal Waterway's the proper name. You've heard of it?"

Dave nodded. This time he said yes.

"Well, there's maybe two thousand feet between there and the beach. Down there right now there're two fine developments started. Houses already going up. Of course, values are different in that section. Prices are higher. Lots start around thirty dollars a foot and go up just as high as you'd want to pay. The ocean front property is all in sound hands but it can be bought, here and there, if a man means business."

He leaned forward suddenly, as though the chair spring had catapulted him. He lowered his voice and smiled.

"Now," he said, "just what was it you had in mind, Mr. Barnum?"

Dave pretended to give the question serious con-sideration. He pursed his lips and frowned.

"It's just a thought I had," he said, "but I was won-dering if there was a motel around that could be bought right, maybe something not too big. It wouldn't have to be too prosperous looking if it could be developed."

"Say no more. I've got the place. Fine location. Owner sort of let it run down but a young man with gumption and some get up and go could do wonders with it."

He stopped and his smile went away, as though his thoughts were finally catching up with his words.

"The only thing is—" He broke off and tried again. "What I mean is, it's funny you should be coming along today like this. Old Ed Greer's had this place on the market for six months. Couldn't get anybody interested. Now this morning he calls up and says he wants to take it off the market for a while. Something about an option."

He hesitated, the enthusiasm oozing from his system. "I suppose I could go down there with you," he said, making no move to get out of his chair.

Dave stood up and said it would not be necessary. He said it might be better if he went alone and looked around without letting Mr. Greer know he was interested in buying.

"If it's anything I'd want and it's still for sale," he said, "I'll stop back."

Bradbery's smile came back. He stood up. The hand that shook Dave's was still warm and damp.

"You do that, Mr. Barnum," he said. "If it doesn't suit you we'll find one that does. Turn left at the light and head south. The first motel you come to is The Plantation. That ain't it. Ed's is the next one. Calls it Villa Greer."

The *Villa Greer* looked just about as Dave expected it to look: weathered, unkempt, ordinary. A fine old banyan tree spread its branches across the front of the property, and opposite its broad trunk stood a small sign which identified the place. There were two stucco units separated by fifty feet of weedy lawn from which grew five or six palm trees of no great distinction. The units— each had four doors with room beside each for a car— seemed solidly constructed but the paint was flecking from the trim. Some of the screens looked rusty, and the benches on the lawn in front of each door also needed paint. A smaller, flat-roofed building stood in line with the right-hand unit but was built apart. The sign which jutted above the doorway said: OFFICE.

Coming in from the sunlight, Dave found the interior dim but surprisingly airy. There was a counter immediately in front of him, a glass case with cigarettes and

gum in it, a rack partly filled with fly-specked postcards
advertising the Villa Greer.

The man who rose from the wicker chair beyond the
counter was tall, gaunt, and round-shouldered. His long
face had a hawklike quality and his thick white hair was
in startling contrast to the wrinkled, sun-browned skin.
He looked to be about sixty-five and his voice had an
unidentifiable twang.

"Something for the night, young man?"

"No," Dave said. "My name's Barnum. I've been looking around and I wanted to make some inquiries about
your place. I understand it's for sale. Is it still on the
market?"

"Yes, and no." Greer leaned his elbows on the
counter. "Yes, it's for sale and no—well, I mean I ain't
sure whether it's on the market now or not. You interested for yourself?"

"Well, in a way."

"You ever been in the motel business?"

"No."

"Know anything about it?"

"Not too much."

"Then let me give you a piece of advice which I don't
expect you to follow but which I'm gonna give you just
the same. Stay out of the motel business. Maybe you
think that's a hell of a way for a man to talk that wants
to sell one."

He stuck out his chin, as though expecting an argument. Dave tried to look impressed. He said he had a
friend who knew more about such things than he did.

"You figure on being partners?" Greer demanded, still
belligerent.

"Well—"

"Are you sure this friend knows the motel business or
is he just talking you into some deal that you may damn
well regret?" He pulled a stubby pipe from his shirt
pocket and reached for the pouch on his hip. "Come
outside," he said.

Dave suppressed a grin. He followed the older man

to a pair of cane chairs in the shade of the banyan. He sat down, knowing he was in for another monologue but willing to listen in return for some information.

"The motel business," Ed Greer said when he had his pipe drawing, "is no place for a young man unless he figures to make a career of it. No damn place for older people either unless they've had some experience along that line. The whole thing is a nasty illusion. It sounds great. Come down here and live all the year round in the sun. In business for yourself, building up for the future, rent free, do the work yourself. You figure all you need, once you've got the capital to get started, is a strong back."

He jabbed his bony chest with the stem of his pipe. "Take me. I'm from Indiana originally. Salaried man most of my life until my father died and left me some property. Mary and I—she was my wife—had been down here a couple of times. Liked it. Hated all that cold weather up north. Not so much the winters as those God damned cold wet springs that never seemed to end."

He made an all-inclusive wave of his pipe. "Helped build this place myself. Had it spick and span. Worked hard, both of us changing sheets and making beds and house cleaning and all that. Made some money, got the place free and clear. It was the paper work got us down. Taxes. Records. Books. State tax, sales tax, room tax, income tax, withholding tax."

He hesitated, mood sobering and his voice full of thought. "I don't know. Maybe I'm just blowing off a head of steam. Maybe if Mary was still alive I'd feel different. Don't seem to give a damn. Don't make the beds any more. Hire it done. Let the place run down and take six dollars a night where I could be getting ten if I'd get to work with some spit and polish and a paintbrush. The trouble is I'm wearing out just like my equipment and I say, the hell with it. That's why I'm selling out when I can. You know what I'm going to do?" he said.

"I'm going to get me a little bungalow over in the
lake country where a man can hunt and fish cheap.
Seven, eight thousand over there will get me the place
I want. I can get sixty for this. Say I can invest fifty at
four per cent. Two thousand a year and only my own
bed to change. Next year I'm getting in on this old-age
pension stuff. Sixty-five. I figure I'll draw sixty-odd dollars a month, enough for taxes on the house and upkeep,
the keep of a second-hand car. Let somebody else worry
about the taxes and keeping the weeds out of the drive
and sendin' back the things these damn-fool tourists
leave in their room and then you have to mail it to them.
I'm tired of bowing and scraping and being polite to
people and listening to their God damned complaints."

He knocked his pipe out in the palm of his hand and
scattered the dottle. He blew through the stem.

"Now this fellow that's interested in my place, it's
different with him. First off he knows his business. An
experienced man. Knows exactly what he's getting into,
knows the only way he could buy this place for sixty
thousand—I've got two hundred feet on the road and
room out back for as many units again as I got, quarter
of a mile to a beach—the only reason he could buy it is
because it's run down. He'll fix that. Paint, new furniture, new sign, neat, attractive grounds will start bringing in ten dollars a night again in the season."

"I think I know the man you mean," Dave said, deciding it was time to get on with what interested him
most. "Stinson?"

"That's right. George Stinson. Runs the Seabeach
Motel up past Vautine. Ambitious, knows how to deal
with people."

"How long has he been interested in this place?"

"For quite a while, on and off. Last month he came
down here and talked real serious. Last week he
dropped in again. That's why I was telling you the place
was off the market, at the moment, but still for sale.
Called me up and asked if I'd take a thousand dollars
for a sixty day option."

"When was that?"

"Last night. Got me out of bed. I asked him why the hell he couldn't wait till morning. Apologized. Said he'd finally made up his mind and wanted my answer."

An odd, tingling sensation grew swiftly in Dave's chest. He found he was unconsciously holding his breath. He let it out easily as he reached for a cigarette.

"What did you tell him?" he asked, not looking up.

"Told him yes. Like to see him get the place because I know how bad he wants it. Called me again this morning and said he was putting the check in the mail. Said he'd stop past in a day or two and sign the agreement."

He turned in his chair as a car pulled off and rolled to a stop near the office.

"If I get the check by morning Stinson's made a deal." He watched a sport-shirted man wearing a long-visored fishing cap unfold himself from the car. "Excuse me," he said. "Time to tend to business."

10

DAVE BARNUM had one more call he wanted to make before dark, and to reach his destination he had to drive forty miles down the coast to this town which stood on an inlet reaching in from the sea. It took a while to make inquiries and get satisfactory directions, and by the time he had turned into the proper road the sun had set and there was only the afterglow to light the land.

Willie Shear's house was one of two which occupied a man-made island. A high stone wall separated it from the neighboring estate, obscuring all but the red-tile roof and running along the front to a concrete retaining wall bordering the water. Steel gates had been swung back to give access to the driveway but as Dave drove

past he noticed a cord-like contrivance had been em-
bedded across the drive, apparently a signaling device
when activated by a passing car.

The house came into view after he had circled for a
hundred feet or so along the black-topped drive and
now, off to the right, he could see the private dock. A
sleek and modern-looking cruiser, which appeared to be
about forty-five feet overall, was moored here, her out-
riggers vertical fingers reaching toward the sky. Working on the brightwork aft was a thick-chested man in
dungarees, T-shirt, and a disreputable-looking yachting
cap.

A four-car garage blocked Dave's view a moment
later and as his glance slid past he brought it swiftly
back to focus on the end car, a robin's-egg-blue convertible with the top down. He knew at once that it
was a Cadillac. He knew too that there undoubtedly
were hundreds like it in that part of the state. Perhaps
it was the association of the car with the name of Willie
Shear that brought to mind the convertible he had seen
pull past him the night before as he ran back to the
bungalow.

He remembered each detail distinctly: the headlights
which had flashed on just as he started to turn into the
grounds, the way the car had angled into the road, its
color and year and model.

Beyond that he could not speculate but now, as he
pulled in behind the two other cars which had been
parked in the drive near the front entrance, he could
feel an odd tension begin to work inside him. When he
stepped to the drive he discovered he was nervous.
Even his thoughts had become apprehensive and uncertain, as though the quiet elegance of the estate had
suddenly taken on some inexplicable but sinister air.

The signaling device at the gate apparently was
working because when he approached the wide front
steps a man awaited him. He wore black, tropical-
weight trousers, and the white jacket of a servant, an
egg-bald, bushy-browed man with a truculent expres-

sion. He looked like a butler, with muscles, but he had none of a butler's air or manner. His gaze was hostile rather than suspicious and he acted as if he found it an effort to be civil.

"Who do you want?" he asked without preliminaries.

"Mr. Shear."

"Who're you?"

"Mr. Barnum. Dave Barnum."

"Mr. Shear know you?"

"Probably not. Just tell him the man who owns the Club 80 wants to see him."

Until then the butler had made up his mind Dave wasn't going to get in. Now he seemed undecided. He turned abruptly and started up the stairs, Dave following. When they reached the top step the fellow stopped and made a downward thrust of his index finger.

"Wait here," he said.

Dave grinned at him. He said: "Thanks." Then, hearing faintly the sound of music, he looked to see where it came from.

There was a picture window on the left of the doorway and because of it he could look through the corner of what appeared to be a living room to the adjacent porch. There was a small bar here, some thickly upholstered chaises and chairs in blue and maroon, an overstuffed divan of the same material. Three women and three men sat around with drinks in their hands and when the butler appeared a moment later one of the men rose and followed him into the living room. Three seconds later the butler reappeared in the doorway.

"In here," he said, and gave a jerk of his head before he disappeared down the hall.

Willie Shear was waiting in the center of a living room that reminded Dave of a composite of all those he had seen in such movies as were devoted to men of Willie's type and profession. His first impression was one of reasonable good taste without distinction—though this may have been the fault of the decorator—an overall air of expensiveness. That was about all he had time for then because Willie Shear was watching him with bright gray eyes that were bored, amused, and, deep down, suspicious.

Dave had not known quite what to expect. He had had a fleeting glimpse of Willie—though he did not know who he was—the day he had called on Gannon, but it was no more than that because Gannon had immediately banished Dave to his own half of the bungalow. His familiarity and knowledge of the more important figures in the gambling world had therefore been limited to newspaper photographers and, as with the living room, Hollywood portrayals of the type. Now he made his own appraisal.

Willie Shear was not formidable in appearance. He did not look particularly tough. He was of average size and might have been in his early forties, more plump than thin, with good shoulders, and not soft looking, at least not in the face and jaw. He was barbered, manicured, and groomed to perfection. He wore what looked to be handmade loafers, fawn-colored cashmere sox, tan doeskin slacks, well pleated and perfectly draped, an off-white shirt of some soft-looking material, and a jacket of navy blue linen that had not yet acquired a wrinkle.

His sportsman's tan seemed to add a distinction of its own so that the only flaw in Willie's appearance was his nose, which had been broken twice and battered frequently in the two years he had battled—with considerable success—for recognition as a welterweight. Having presently discovered easier ways of making a living, he now had this souvenir as the only reminder of that phase of his life, and somehow that lopsided nose seemed to add rather than detract from his appearance. It was honorably earned and lent character and a certain rugged authority to a face that might otherwise have been simply dismissed as ordinary.

All in all it seemed to Dave that if there was to be one adjective to be used concerning his impression of Willie Shear, that word would have to be "successful" regardless of his business, background, or breeding.

"Leroy said the name was Barnum." Willie's voice was like the rest of him, confident, assured, a bit superior. "Dave Barnum."

"That's right," Dave said, and grinned, not at Willie but at the butler's name.

"And what was that about owning the Club 80?"

"That's also right."

Suspicion flicked again in the gray eyes.

"John Gannon owned the 80."

"He was murdered last night."

"So I heard. A Captain Vaughn from up in Vantine was down here a couple of hours ago with one of the local boys." Willie's glance slid away and his voice grew quiet. "A tough break," he said. "Gannon was one of the old-timers. A big name in his day. I knew him well. What about the funeral? I'd like to send flowers. . . . You own the Club 80 now?" he said with a swiftness of digression that surprised Dave. "How does that happen?"

"I inherited it."

It was Willie's turn to register surprise. He tipped his head forward an inch and his lids went down and up like shades. Then, apparently convinced by something in Dave's manner, he shrugged.

"Related?"

"No."

"An old friend?"

"Of my father's. He helped me through college. There weren't any relatives and—" Dave checked the sentence because the thought of John Gannon and that will bothered him greatly. "He also named me executor."

"Is that what you wanted to talk to me about?"

"Yes."

"Why?"

"I understood you wanted to buy it."

"Who said so?"

"John. You were up there the day before yesterday talking terms, weren't you? You and Sam Resnik."

Dave had let his glance stray even as he spoke. It was

difficult not to. For almost the entire wall separating
the living room from the screened and covered porch
was glass, and to Dave the three women who sat outside were something to see.

Two were blonde, one a brunette. All were smartly
dressed, all were young, all were exceedingly shapely
and apparently quite well aware of the fact. Dave had
an idea that it would take a good hour to make them up
the way they were but he also guessed that if you had
a pocketful of money and an evening to spare a man
would find any one of them attentive.

The two men looked younger than Willie. Their
jackets were too natty and too loud but they looked all
right considering the company they kept. Both were
dark complected and Dave wondered if some of this
darkness came from inheritance rather than the sun.
The one with the taller of the two blondes was holding
her hand in a careless way as he sat beside her on the
divan; the other was busy talking to the second blonde
who sat at his feet on the chaise. Dave couldn't hear
the words but the gestures supported the impression.

When, a moment later, he looked at Willie Shear he
could tell the other was aware of his interest and he
found the open amusement in Willie's eyes embarrassing. Willie allowed himself a small grin and nodded.

"You're right about wanting to buy. The thing is"—he
looked out on the porch—"we were going out in a few
minutes. For a drink or two and a spot of dinner. Why
don't you come along, Barnum? Then after dinner maybe we could have a talk."

Dave's laugh sounded a bit forced, even to him. He
said he guessed not, but thanks just the same. He said
it looked like a case of six being company and seven a
crowd.

"I can fix that," Willie said. "I can have someone over
here for you in fifteen minutes."

"Thanks just the same."

"I think you'd like her. In fact I'd guarantee it. A very

luscious number." He hesitated, still amused. "If you're worrying about the tab—"

Dave said he wasn't worried. He was annoyed at Willie's amusement but he did not say so. He said he wasn't dressed for it, that he had to get back.

"All right." Willie glanced at his watch. "Let's go in here."

He led the way back to the hall and along it to a room on the left, a paneled room filled with books and leather furniture. He stepped to a cellarette and lifted the top to expose bottles, glasses, an ice bucket. He asked what Dave would have.

"Nothing, thanks."

Willie shrugged with his eyebrows, then came round behind a walnut desk and eased down in his executive's chair. He took out an ebony cigarette holder trimmed with gold and began to fit a cigarette into it. When he was satisfied he spun a light from a table lighter.

As he settled back to inhale, the breeze coming through the window ruffled the papers on the desk. He shifted a silver ash tray so it would serve as a paper-weight and during this time Dave had a chance to do some thinking. He was impressed by Willie Shear and he knew it. He had an idea it would be a mistake to underestimate Willie and he suspected that most of those who had done so had cause to regret it.

At the moment he himself had no intention of trying to outsmart the man. Somehow he felt that to do so would put him beyond his depth. The first intuitive warning that there was something sinister about the house had long since vanished but that same sort of intuition warned him to be cautious now. He wanted information and he hoped that by the right sort of cross-questioning and the proper pretense he could get it.

"I understand you were willing to pay $120,000 for the property," he said.

"Something like that. If Gannon had been alive on the first of the month I'd have had myself a new club."

"I'm a little surprised that you'd want it."

"Why?"

"You're a big operator."

"Who said so?"

"Several people."

Willie was not displeased. He examined his cigarette holder.

"If the Club 80 was mine it would be bigger," he said matter-of-factly. "There's plenty of room. A little re-modeling would fix it so I could double the size of that gambling room. I'd double the number of customers too."

He tapped ashes, put the holder in his mouth, and spoke past it.

"Sam was smart enough to give his customers good food. I'd keep that but I'd put a real orchestra in there, some real top entertainers. By next season I'd be able to triple the profits. That's my business."

"If you had bought it, or could buy it," Dave said, "how would Resnik come out?"

"With get-away money. That's about all. Sam made a bad deal when he made that agreement with Gannon. The way I understand it, the only thing Sam could get out of it if Gannon sold to someone else or refused to renew the lease was what wasn't built into the property: his gambling equipment, the tables, chairs, probably some of the kitchen stuff. All the rest of it is part of the building—the booths, bandstand, bar—and he'd be lucky to salvage ten G's."

He glanced beyond Dave into some remoteness of his own and said: "Until a week or so ago there was a chance Sam might meet my offer. With what he had in his hand then plus what he could borrow he might have swung it because I'd made up my mind not to go much higher. The trouble was he ran into a run of the wheel that damn near broke him."

"I heard about that too," Dave said.

Willie's gray glance came back and focused. He waved the cigarette holder.

"But what's the point in all this chatter? You may own

the Club 80—the property—but as I understood that agreement, Sam still has the concession. He can buy— or could if he had the scratch—or he can continue to lease from you. So where are we?"

It was Dave's chance to carry the ball and he concentrated on the impression he hoped to make. His suggestion had no basis in fact but Willie did not know this, and so Dave talked to him as he would to a jury, with assurance and conviction. His dark-blue gaze was steady, his voice firm.

"I'm a lawyer, Mr. Shear," he said. "The key to this thing is the agreement. What I came here for is to find out if, in the event the agreement could be broken, you'd still be interested in buying."

Dave got his reaction. Willie sat up, his eyes narrowed and attentive.

"Could it?" he said quietly.

"Could it what?"

"Be broken."

"I don't know."

Suspicion flared in the narrowed gaze and a tightness grew around the thin mouth.

"You said you were a lawyer. You've seen the agreement."

Dave had most of the information he had come for. He should have been satisfied to walk out and let it go at that. But having created an impression, even though it was a false one, he had to wind it up in proper fashion. He pushed back in his chair. He spread his hands.

"Once," he said. "I read it. It seemed in order. But at that time Gannon was alive and I had no idea that I was named in his will. To know whether an agreement can be broken you have to read it paragraph by paragraph, line by line, word by word. It takes time. I don't know that it's worth it."

With that, as startling as they were unexpected, two things happened, one after the other. Willie Shear was snubbing the butt out of his cigarette holder and he moved the ash tray again, enough so that the top half of the papers heretofore secured riffled in the breeze. That was when Dave saw the top copy of the agreement, not the one between Gannon and Resnik but the simple one he had drawn the afternoon before the murder.

He was looking right at it as the breeze pinned it there. He recognized it because he had drawn it. He knew instantly that the last time he had seen it was when Gannon put it in the safe.

Simultaneously Willie was on his feet and turning toward a small oil painting between the bookcases. Instead of hanging in normal fashion the frame was hinged, and when Willie lifted it, it stayed parallel with the floor to reveal a wall safe much like Gannon's.

Willie opened it, took out a thick sheaf of bills. Not bothering to close the safe he turned and tossed the bills on the desk. They were hundred-dollar bills held together with an inch-wide paper band. Initialed there in ink were the letters T.A.K.

For the next second or two Dave could only stare. It was impossible for him to hide completely the shock of his discovery. *The agreement and the same five thousand dollars Gannon had once let him hold. The blue car outside the motel last night.*

These were the only things he could think of as the sudden excitement hammered at his senses. When he looked up Willie was smiling at him but it was a smile without suspicion and Dave understood that Willie accepted the reaction as one of surprise rather than excited recognition. Dave concentrated on his voice to keep it casual.

"What's that for?" he asked, nodding at the bills.

"Call it earnest money, if you want. While you're checking over that old agreement. If you think you can break it you've got some option money."

"Suppose I can't break it?"

"Why then"—Willie grinned but his inflection was unmistakable—"I think you'd better bring it back. Less, say, ten per cent for your trouble. Fair enough?"

Dave reached for the bills. He put them in his pocket

and took out a cigarette. When he had a light he reached toward the ash tray with the burnt match.

What he did then was probably not very bright. If he had been ten years older and more experienced he most likely would not even have made the attempt. As it was there was all this excitement working on him and not much time to think things through. Instead he was concentrating on such things as odds and opportunity, and together they seemed to add up in his favor. The rest of it was simply impulse.

"I think I will have that drink," he said as calmly as he could. "A light Bourbon if it's handy."

Willie turned to the cellarette. He poured whisky into a glass, standing in profile so that Dave was still afraid to make a direct attempt to get the agreement. Had it been on top he might have done so but as it was he moved the ash tray and the breeze came in on cue.

Papers started to skitter across the desk and from there to the floor. The agreement, clipped to its carbon, came into view and Dave reached for it along with some other sheets, dropping to his knees behind the desk as though to retrieve still more.

His hands hidden from sight, he managed to fold the agreement roughly and stuff it inside the waistband of his trousers under his jacket. When he straightened he had a half dozen sheets in his hand. He stacked them and put them back under the ash tray, apologizing for his clumsiness.

Willie put the highball on the desk and retrieved the rest of the papers which had been blown out of Dave's reach. He said it did not matter, and put them under the ash tray.

Dave drank his highball standing. It was short and strong and he needed it badly. Then Willie was smiling, taking his elbow in friendly fashion and leading him from the room and along the hall. As they came to the living-room door he stopped and looked across it to the porch. The dusk was thickening now but those outside were still visible: the two on the divan, the couple on the chaise who had drawn closer, the brunette, apparently Willie's girl, sitting alone and pouting.

"Sure you won't change your mind, Barnum?" he said. "She's a redhead. Very nice." He grinned. "Or maybe you think I can't deliver."

"I'm sure you can," Dave said, his nerves jumping and his laugh forced. "Maybe some other time."

"Any time," Willie said, still highly amused. He walked to the front steps. "Let me hear from you," he said, and turned back into the house.

Dave went down the steps stiffly, his muscles tight all over. He was never in a greater hurry and yet he forced himself to stroll easily along the drive in the half-light, past the two parked cars to his own. He found his keys, glanced idly about in case anyone was looking, and climbed in.

Before he turned on the ignition he switched the folded agreement from his waistband to his inside pocket. Then he started the engine, pulled out into the drive, and circled back to the straightaway leading to the gate.

He flicked on his parking lights and touched the accelerator lightly. He was never sure whether he actually heard the sound of the alarm or not. He was quite sure that there was no one in the drive, no one near the gates. Yet even as he approached them he saw them start to swing.

He was then about forty feet away and now the panic hit him as he understood what was happening. He stepped hard on the throttle and the car bucked ahead. He leaned over the wheel, gripping it hard as though to help it forward while the perspiration broke out all over him.

Actually he never had a chance and he knew it even then. The gates were swinging too fast and the bars were too solid looking. The gap narrowed so swiftly he had no choice but to jam on the brakes. When he skidded to a stop there was a space of about two feet between his bumper and the steel bars.

11

FOR ANOTHER three or four seconds Dave Barnum
sat perfectly still while the panic gave way to a strange
sort of fear. It was not so much the things he had done
that motivated this fear as it was the uncanny way those
gates had blocked his escape and locked him securely in
Willie Shear's domain.

He switched on his headlights but they did not help
much in the gathering darkness. The gates stood out
silent and formidable, representing the power of the
man who had had them installed. The thought of this
gave him a trapped and hopeless feeling and he accepted the thought that to make any attempt at escape
would be futile.

Then, suddenly, he chuckled aloud and the fear was
gone. There was nothing sinister about the house. There
was nothing sinister about Willie. Willie was a big
operator and he had to take precautions against those
who tried to outsmart him. A guy named Dave Barnum
had made his play and muffed it like the amateur he
was. Now it was Willie's turn to deal the cards.

The sound of running footsteps came to interrupt such
thoughts and presently the door next to him opened
and the thick-chested man in the T-shirt and yachting
cap slid in on the seat beside him. At the same time a
rear door opened and when Dave glanced around he
saw a slim youth in a chauffeur's uniform.

"Back up, bud," T-shirt said. "The boss wants a word
with you."

Dave backed up until he was opposite the front steps.
He cut the motor and the lights. When he slid from
behind the wheel the chauffeur was right beside him
and T-shirt was coming round to join them. Together
and without a word they entered the house. The party

was still going on out on the porch and no one paid
them the slightest attention as they moved down the
hall and into the study.

Willie Shear was standing, a fresh cigarette in his
holder. He looked Dave over and smiled, his gaze
speculative over the flame as he puffed the cigarette
alight.

Dave grinned back, an unexpected anger beginning
to germinate somewhere inside him. He said that was
quite a gate Willie had.

"Yeah," Willie said. "Cute." He glanced at his two
employees and dipped his head in command. "Search
him!"

They reached for Dave and the anger that had only
just begun to blossom erupted violently. There was
nothing premeditated about the reaction and it was
probably born of frustration. The roughness with which
T-shirt spun him around may have been the final con-
tributing factor but it was the festering rancorous
thought of failure after having been so near success that
was at fault.

T-shirt was rough and Dave was young and proud
and he was not used to being handled that way. He
did not consider the consequences nor, at the moment,
did he give a damn about Willie Shear.

He spun round easily, hooking a solid, well-timed
left smack against a blunt, bewhiskered jaw and, still
moving in, laid on a right.

They pleased him, those punches. He exulted in the
shock that ran clear to his shoulders. He was elated
with the results that knocked the face right out from
under the disreputable yachting cap.

T-shirt might have gone down if he hadn't stumbled
back against a chair and caught his balance. But that
was all. Before Dave could turn, something hard hit
him in the small of the back and the party was over.

"*All right!*"

The voice was Willie's, commanding and incisive.
Dave stood still and the quiet grew around him.

"I don't like rough stuff," Willie said. "Pick up your cap, Saul. Now search him!"

Saul flexed his jaw from side to side and his eyes were mean. He put on his hat and stepped close, the eyes daring Dave to make another move. He searched with swift efficiency and put Dave's wallet, the agreement, and the five thousand dollars on the desk.

"No gun," he said and with that the hard round pressure on Dave's spine was withdrawn.

"Outside," Willie said and stood waiting until Saul and the chauffeur had gone. Then he slid a doeskinned thigh across the corner of the desk and gave Dave his attention. He took his time, his gray eyes hard and probing. Finally he picked up the wallet and handed it back. After another moment he reached for the telephone.

"You're a lawyer," he said. "Would you say that play of yours added up to larceny?"

Dave stared at him, uncomprehending. He glanced down at the five thousand dollars and then at the agreement.

"What did I steal, a sheet of paper?"

"And five thousand bucks."

"Wait a minute," Dave said. "You gave me that money."

"Who says so besides you? . . . I don't operate in this precinct. The cops and I are pals. If I call them in now they'll believe what I tell them. They'll take you down. If I say so you'll spend the night in the jug. If you don't think so you can name your odds."

Dave moved a step closer, his bony face darkly scowling and his feelings outraged and incensed. But he had been well trained in law school and he could think on his feet. The look he gave Willie was mildly contemptuous.

"I wouldn't take that bet at any odds, Willie," he said, using the name for the first time. "Because I've a hunch you could swing it. But if you want a bet I'll give you one: even money that you won't."

Willie balanced the telephone on his thigh, half-closing one eye. "Won't what?" he said.

"Won't put in that call."

"Why?"

"Even money," Dave said and reached into his pocket. "But something I can afford. Say ten dollars." He put the bill on the desk.

Willie looked at it and stood up, for this was language he understood. He produced a thick fold of bills. He had a hard time finding anything smaller than a fifty but he finally discovered a twenty. He put it down and pushed the ten aside.

"You got a bet," he said. "Why?"

"Because to make the charge stick you'd have to offer the money and agreement as evidence of larceny. You'd be a sucker to take the chance after all the trouble you went to, to get them back from Gannon."

Willie considered the words, his eyes busy with thought. He glanced down at the telephone he had put aside. When he looked up again there was something new showing through the surface hardness. It might have been an incipient smile; it might have been respect.

"You're an almost smart guy, Barnum," he said finally. "You had me fooled right up to the end. I'm still a little fooled, but I'll get down to that later. On this one you win." He picked up the ten and pushed the twenty toward Dave. He went round the desk to his chair and sat down.

"In my business a guy develops sort of a sixth sense," he said as Dave picked up the twenty with a word of thanks. "He has to if he's going to stay near the top. I don't know what you'd call it, maybe some sort of acquired instinct, but you either have it or you don't last long. You learn to spot a phony, and a phony move. You finally made one but it took me a minute to spot it. Moving that ash tray, the papers blowing just when my back was turned." He shook his head. "Not good, Barnum. Up to then, yes. When I found out what was missing, it was a cinch. The gate operates from here."

He nodded at the chair Dave had used before. "Sit down," he said. "Let's get back to that remark about my taking the trouble to get this stuff back from Gannon. How do you know? Or are you guessing?"

"I saw your car," Dave said, taking a chance. "Last night outside the Seabeach Motel."

Willie never batted an eye, for he too had been well trained.

"Yeah?" he said. "What's the license number?"

Very good, Dave thought. *Oh, very good indeed.* Then, because he'd lost that round, he said:

"I'm the one who drew that agreement. The top copy was in Gannon's safe the day before yesterday. I saw him put it there along with that five thousand in hundreds. I know because I recognized the initials on the band."

He hesitated, having Willie's complete attention now. "From then on I was with, or near, Cannon practically all the time. Right up until an hour or so before he was killed. So how did you get them, Willie? If it wasn't your car outside?"

Willie nodded. There was no change in his expression but somehow he seemed satisfied. He broke the paper band on the bills and put it in the ash tray. He sparked flame from the table lighter and watched it consume the band. When he had torn the two agreement sheets he put them in the ash tray and repeated the process. He stirred the ashes with his fingertip and leaned back.

"What've you got now, Barnum?"

Dave started to get up. As he had originally suspected, he was just a little out of his depth here. Aware that there was nothing more to be said, he was ready to go, if he could. Willie had not quite finished.

"Almost smart," he said thoughtfully. "A very good performance. Using that gag of suggesting Resnik's agreement might be broken was clever. You conned me nicely." He put his hand on the edge of the desk, as though about to rise. "You're spoiling my dinner party, Barnum," he said. "I'm late now so I'll ask you one more

question and if I think I've got a level answer the meet-
ing can adjourn."

He hesitated again. "You didn't come here because
of the agreement or the five grand, because you didn't
know I had 'em until you saw 'em. So what brought you
here in the beginning? A hunch? The car?"

"Information. I wanted information," Dave said.

"About what?"

"Sam Resnik. The sort of deal he had and how he
stood. I figured you'd know more about that than anyone else."

Apparently Willie decided to accept the answer. He
stood up. "Get what you wanted?" he asked in a voice
that suggested he did not much care.

"I've got more now than I had when I came."

"You've still got your health too," Willie said. "That's
more than some can say who take a swing at Saul. . . .
Come on," he said. "It's getting late but I think I could
still get that redhead for you if you're interested."

They were opposite the living room now, and outside
the porch was lighted. The tall blonde and her man
were in a careless embrace. On the chaise the other
blonde was sitting on her companion's lap but he was
still talking. Willie's girl, the brunette, was no longer
pouting, she was furious.

Dave shook his head. He grinned because he could
not help it. "No thanks," he said. He went down the
steps without glancing back. When he rolled the car
down the driveway the gate was open.

Betty Nelson had a very pleasant afternoon with her
Boothville friend, Joyce. They had dinner in an inex-
pensive restaurant that had a tea-room atmosphere and
made a specialty of pastries, on which they gorged
themselves. They went to a movie which featured Greg-
ory Peck and pleased them both. Now, over their drugstore sodas, the gossip continued. Not, however, about
old times and college friends. For Joyce had read of the

murder in the *Boothville Standard* and what she wanted was details, and more details.

In later years it was likely that Joyce would have a figure which would be classified as dumpy, but right now she was a sturdy, vital-looking girl with reddish-brown hair, a hearty laugh, and a bright, ingenuous manner. She had been Betty's roommate in the college dormitory their freshman year and they had both made the same sorority where the friendship continued. It was partly because of her—she was a native of Booth-ville—that Betty had taken this job in the South.

That afternoon on the beach she had listened to such facts of murder as Betty could supply, and then had asked for character sketches of the principals together with their dossiers. She had asked for Betty's own suspicions and when none were forthcoming had brought forth some of her own. Now, over the last of their sodas, she was ready with her opinion.

"I think it was Tyler," she said.

"Why?"

"Because he's the only one that didn't know Mr. Gannon had tried to commit suicide."

"Maybe he did know and we don't know it." Betty remained unconvinced. "And anyway, Mr. Gannon wasn't shot to make it look like suicide."

"Just the same," Joyce said, "I think he's the one. Running away with Mr. Gannon's daughter and killing her and then having the nerve to come back to ask for money. Now he's going to get it. . . . Wait and see," she said when they walked out of the store, "if I'm not right."

Betty laughed as they walked along the sidewalk to her car. Joyce laughed too, but more reservedly. When they had embraced in their usual fashion and Betty had promised to let her know of any new developments, Joyce voiced her warning. She said Betty should be careful.

"You're a sort of witness, you know," she said. "Whoever killed Mr. Gannon might kill again if he had to."

Betty wanted to tell her friend she had been seeing too many crime pictures but she didn't. She said she would be careful and promptly forgot the matter as she concentrated on the business of driving through the town.

She had always tried to maintain what, for that part of the country, might be called a conservative speed. When she thought to look at the speedometer she tried to keep the needle between forty-five and fifty, and at that most of the traffic passed her by. Lights bothered her sometimes and she was glad that there was so little traffic tonight.

An occasional car overtook her and then pulled out to speed past, but there had been no trailer-trucks, which always made her nervous with the roar and suction of their passing. There was a car behind her now as she came to this deserted stretch of road where the highway was elevated and ran for a mile or more through a swampy lowland studded with stumps and stunted trees.

Keeping well to her own side of the road she waited for the car to pass. She glanced at the headlights in the rearview mirror and when they finally angled out behind her she concentrated on holding the wheel straight, not looking at the car as it drew ahead but letting up slightly on the accelerator as a safety measure.

It was probably that as much as anything that saved her, for if she had maintained her speed the other car, drawing ahead and then swerving sharply right to crowd her off the road, would have clipped her more solidly.

Even so she saw the crash coming. Disaster threatened and what she did then was automatic, and born of instinct and healthy reflexes. In that first terrifying, fantastic moment she could only wrench at the wheel. Then as her headlights swept the empty blackness of the swamp and the car started to skid with the application of her brakes, she fought that skid and let the brakes alone.

Somehow the car remained upright. Somehow she was able to cling to the wheel. Even as the coupe hung there on the brink she managed to step on the gas. Miraculously then the car rocked back on four wheels. Canted at a crazy angle the tires gained traction. The car bucked, wheels churning. It rocked back. Then, at what seemed like the final instant, it climbed the edge of the bank before it shuddered into a stall with its front wheels on the highway.

Betty sat where she was, too weak and helpless to find the starter button, afraid to move lest the car roll backward. A trailer-truck thundered at her from behind and she heard the hiss of air as the brakes were applied. Seconds later a shadowy figure appeared at the door, opening it now, muttering curses in the instant before it spoke.

"I wish to God I could get my hands on that guy," the voice said. Then, more gently: "I think you'd better get out, miss. I can snag you out of here in a jiffy."

Betty moved automatically, vaguely aware that the driver had a helper who was lighting a flare to warn oncoming traffic. Cars came and slowed down and passed, their occupants peering out the windows. The truck reversed slowly and in a matter of minutes a towing cable had been attached and the coupe was back on the road.

The driver got in and started it. He said it seemed to be all right and did Betty think she'd be able to drive. She said yes because she knew she had to drive. She got in and shifted, disciplining her nerves as best she could. She voiced her thanks and the driver waved to her as he put the truck in motion.

12

DAVE BARNUM was too occupied with his encounter
with Willie Shear to realize he was hungry until he had
driven nearly twenty miles. Then, seeing the lights of
a roadside restaurant ahead of him, he pulled in, and in
the space of thirty minutes, including time of prepara-
tion, demolished a steak sandwich and three cups of
coffee.

It was after ten when he drove through Vantine, and
without any intention of stopping at the Club 80 he
found himself heading for the parking lot. By the time
he was inside he knew he wanted a drink so he stopped
at the bar and ordered his Bourbon and water. Beyond,
in the main room, the orchestra was playing and he saw
Liza Drake sitting with some people at a table. Apparently she saw him too because she appeared at his side
when he was about halfway through his drink. He said
hello, and what would she have?

"Nothing, thanks."

Liza looked very striking in the white, strapless gown
that contrasted so sharply with her tanned shoulders.
It fitted her handsome, full-blown body like a sheath,
and it was obvious that there was very little but Liza
underneath. Her red mouth held a faint and none too
reassuring smile, and her dark eyes, black in the shadows, were enigmatic as they inspected him.

Dave waited, aware that she had something on her
mind that concerned him and not particularly wanting
to hear it. Neither did he intend to gulp his drink and
run. Presently she had her say.

"Your friend was around to see me," she said.

"Friend?"

"Captain Vaughn."

Oh, thought Dave, *so that's it.*

He considered again his earlier estimate of the woman and decided she would be a swell person to have on your side. She would be a staunch and loyal supporter so long as she liked you. Having earned her displeasure, as he most certainly had, you would find things less pleasant.

"Why don't you ask me what he wanted?" she asked coldly. "Sleeping capsules," she added when Dave kept his attention on his drink.

"Did he find any?"

"No."

"He didn't think he would."

"He asked me what I'd done with them. I told him I never used them." She hesitated, her smile fixed. "He quoted you. I said no. It was sort of a standoff."

In trying to avoid her gaze, Dave's glance slid beyond her to find Sam Resnik picking his way through the tables, and now it came to him that, at the moment, he had no more desire to talk to Sam than to Liza. Very quickly then he put a bill on the bar. He said good night and walked out.

Dave saw Betty's car when he rolled down the driveway. He parked his own car, locked the doors, and came round to the front of the bungalow. As he entered and snapped on the lights he heard Betty call to him.

A sudden glow of pleasure struck through him in that first instant when he stepped to the door and saw her on the steps. "Hi," he said. "Have a good time?"

He did not get at all the reaction he expected. When he stepped outside and took her hand he could feel it tremble. He detected a certain breathlessness in her voice when she spoke.

"I think," she said, "I need a drink. I've been waiting for you to come."

The words jarred him but he sensed that this was not the time for questions.

"Sure."

He drew her into the bungalow and here, where the light was good, he could see the traces of shock in the

corners of her hazel eyes. Her face was still pale under
its film of moisture and though he understood at once
that something had happened he wanted to get some
of the drink into her before any sign of hysteria could
develop. He tried to play it lightly.

"Should we pull the blinds? In case Mrs. Craft has
her binoculars out?"

She shook her head, her small smile forced. "I think
it would be better to leave them up. Then Mrs. Craft
won't have to use her imagination."

He made the drinks quickly, handing her the stronger
one. He insisted that she drink half of it before he con-
sented to listen. Then, standing in front of her chair, he
heard her story.

Even now it scared him a little because her own fears
were so real, the details so vivid. But the talking had
helped her. There was a calmness about her voice and
manner that reassured him. The color had seeped back
into her cheeks and he could see her facial muscles compose themselves one by one. When he questioned her
about certain details she answered as best she could but
when, finally, he asked if she thought the attempt could
have been deliberate, she could not say.

"I simply don't know," she said. "I thought about it
all the way back and while I was waiting for you to
come. I told myself it was ridiculous to build things up
in my mind. Things like that happen all the time."

Dave agreed. He said it might have been a drunken
driver, or some crazy kid who had misjudged the distance in passing. He told himself it was a risk you had
to take when you drove a car. She had been lucky, but
she was safe, and what more could one ask?

It was all very sound thinking. The trouble was he
did not believe it. When she finally decided it could
not have been deliberate, that there was no reason for
it, he had to disagree.

"Did you see the car?" he asked. "Anything about it—
kind or style or size?"

"No, I hardly saw it."

"If it was deliberate," he said, thinking aloud, "who-ever did it would have to know you were going to Boothville. He'd have to keep an eye on you and be ready to follow you home. A smart guy wouldn't take a chance on using his own car. He'd rent one or steal one. . . . Resnik's got plenty of tough help down at the club," he continued. "He has to have in that busi-ness. He'd know how to get a car. He wouldn't even have to do it himself."

"But why should he—"

He cut her off more sharply than he intended. "You saw him outside here last night. You're the only one that saw him."

She said: "O-hh!" and her eyes went wide.

"Who else could it be?" he asked, quiet now but per-sistent. "What else did you see that you haven't told me?"

"Nothing."

"Think." He watched her shake her head and then remembered something else. "Did you see a Cadillac convertible around here at any time after you and Workman came back? A blue one?"

"I—I don't think so. No, I'm sure I didn't."

"And what about Workman? How long did it take you to change into your bathing suit after he left you?"

"I don't know. I just—well—"

"Five minutes?"

"Probably. I undressed and hung up my things and put my suit on and pinned up my hair. I checked to see if I had cigarettes in my beach bag."

"Were you ready when he came? Did you have to wait?"

Her brow furrowed with thought, the frown reaching down into the saddle of freckles on the bridge of her nose.

"Maybe a minute or two. But you don't think Carl—"

She refused to finish the thought and Dave said he did not know what to think. In his own mind he was sure of only two things: he was badly confused, and he was worried about Betty. He glanced at his watch. He said it might be a little late to call Captain Vaughn but he'd try.

The operator at the police station said the captain wasn't in and Dave said if he could be reached to tell him that Dave Barnum had called. Then he made Betty finish her drink. He walked her to her room. When he insisted that he go in with her and glance around she giggled.

"What," she said, "will Mrs. Craft think now?"

The remark that came first to his mind was too profane to repeat so he settled for a grunt. "I'll give Mrs. Craft something else to think about," he said and then, standing there in the doorway, he kissed her.

It was a thing he had not attempted before and he acted now on impulse alone. She looked so lovely standing there and looking up at him that he leaned down before she knew what was happening, pressing her lips lightly with his own because it was something he simply had to do.

"Lock the door," he said, and pressed her hand. "I'll take this up with Mrs. Craft in the morning."

He stepped back into darkness before she could reply and he stood there until the door closed and the lock clicked into place. When he got back to his own place the telephone was ringing and the familiar voice of Captain Vaughn came to him as he answered.

Vaughn listened to the story without comment. When it was over he asked the same questions Dave had asked Betty.

"It could have been an accident," he said finally, "the way the screwballs drive these days, but thanks for telling me. I'll see what I can find. I'll want to see you in the morning, too."

"All right," Dave said, "but make it late. I've got some things to do."

"Like what?"

"I'm expecting a copy of the will. I'll have to come in

and talk to some people about taxes and death certifi-
cates and property values and funeral arrangements."

Vaughn said he saw what Dave meant. He said he
would expect him as soon as he could make it.

Dave Barnum seldom saw any of the transient customers of the Seabeach Motel at breakfast. On the days
when he had gone fishing with Gannon they had been
away too early, and at other times the transients were
gone when Dave got to the Coffee Shop. It was that
way this morning, or nearly so.

Two cars stood outside the door, one with Michigan
plates and one from Ohio. Both were well laden and
when he went inside one man was picking his teeth
while he waited for change and his wife took a post-
card from the counter. Another family group of four
was just getting up from the counter. Other than that
there was only one other customer, a woman of thirty
or perhaps a bit more, with auburn hair and considerable make-up for that hour of the morning. Her brows
were arched and penciled, her mouth dark red against
her city-white complexion. Sitting down she seemed
tall and thin, and she wore an expensive-looking sun
suit which seemed a little brief for one about to face a
day of travel.

Betty led him to his usual table and the quick bright
smile she gave him was of a very special sort that he
had never seen before. It did things to her hazel eyes
that was wonderful to behold as she handed him the
menu.

"Mrs. Craft was in," she said in a conspiratorial whisper. "She didn't say a thing."

"She'd better not." He dipped his head toward the
woman in the sun suit. "Something new?"

"She came yesterday afternoon after I'd left. She's in
number 3, I think."

"Umm," said Dave.

"Um, yourself," Betty said as she moved away.

Carl Workman cleared up the mystery a few minutes
later. He arrived while Dave was eating his grapefruit,
looking very natty in light-gray trousers, white shoes,
and one of his short-sleeved shirts, a plain dark blue
this time. He winked at Dave as he caught his eye, but
he turned immediately to the woman's table.

He smiled. He said good morning. Dave could not
hear what the woman said but he saw her smile in profile and Workman said something else. Then he was
sitting down opposite her and signaling a waitress.

The woman was already on her coffee when Workman's juice came but she stayed to smoke a cigarette.
After about ten minutes she left, Workman watching
the swinging hips with approval before he picked up
his coffee and joined Dave.

"I'm retiring from competition," he said in his quick,
incisive way. He nodded, his amber eyes amused and a
smile working at the corners of his thin mouth. "From
now on you can have a clear field and a fast track."

"With what?"

"With Betty."

"Good," Dave said. "That's damn nice of you."

"I knew you'd appreciate it. You saw the number that
just left?"

"I did."

"The Widow Collins. I spent most of last evening
trying to make a little time. She's decided to stay a few
days."

Dave studied the tanned, hard-jawed face, his
thoughts not entirely on what Workman said. He noticed the way the thinning hair grew in a widow's peak
from the bony forehead, and then the amber gaze held
his and he made an appropriate answer. He said Workman's decision would be a great shock to Betty.

"She'll get over it," the other said, still grinning, "with
your help. With Betty I found myself unable to make
even an innocent pass, which was not my nature. I'm
hoping," he added, "that the widow will appreciate my
talents."

For a moment then Dave considered telling Workman about Betty's near accident because it had been
his opinion right along that here was a shrewd, tough-
fibered man, competent and experienced. Yet even as
the thought came to him he knew that from now on,
where Betty was concerned, he could trust no one. He
picked up his check and left a tip.

"If the widow needs a reference," he said, "send her
to me."

"I'll do that," Workman said. "Where you off to?"

"Town. A copy of the will came this morning. I've
got a lot of things to do. Also," he said, "Captain
Vaughn wants to see me."

"Yeah, Vaughn." Workman's smile went away. "He
hasn't bothered me since yesterday morning. I hope it
stays that way. . . . See you on the beach, Kid."

13

IT WAS eleven o'clock before Dave could get to Captain Vaughn's and by that time he felt pretty low. It had
not been a pleasant morning even though he got co-
operation wherever he went.

He had stopped first at the funeral parlor. Here the
owner told him he would arrange to get a copy of the
death certificate and take care of the details, but even
so Dave had to select an appropriate casket and arrange
for shipping the body back to Somerville where he had
learned Gannon's family had a plot.

When he had talked to Boston to explain what he had
done and ask for advice, he went to the county building
to discuss the business aspects of the estate with the
proper officials, and then he had to call Boston again
and inform the office of the situation. He was in the tax
collector's office, and had not yet been to the bank,
when Vaughn phoned to remind him to stop in. He had

promised to do so within the next half hour, and now
he sank gratefully into the chair beside the captain's
desk and wiped the perspiration from his face and forehead.

Vaughn let him take his time. He was leaning back
in his chair, looking cool and unruffled in his shirt
sleeves and cotton trousers, but his dark eyes were sym-
pathetic because he knew what Dave had been through.

"I haven't been able to do a thing on that accident
business," he said finally. "Doubt if I will. You got any
idea why anyone—except maybe Resnik—would want
the girl out of the way?"

Dave shook his head. He said no and Vaughn went
on to other things. He said he had called on Liza Drake.

"She told me," Dave said. "She said you didn't find
capsules."

"Didn't figure to with the swamps so handy. I told
her what you said. She said you'd told her the same
thing and she didn't know what you were talking
about." He gestured emptily.

"That seems to be that—for now. But there's another
little matter I'd like to discuss. This capsule business
isn't the only thing you held out on me." He paused,
gaze steady, letting his words sink in. "Had a visit with
a Mrs. Craft," he said. "A guest up at your motel. Said
she'd given you some information."

Dave remembered. He also realized that in the light
of what he now knew about Stinson the information
could be important.

"Mrs. Craft," he said by way of excuse, "is a gossip.
She's a busybody."

"Gossips see things. Mrs. Craft saw Stinson going
toward Gannon's place around eleven or so."

"She didn't see him go in."

"No."

Vaughn's gaze remained steady, and more speculative than hostile. "It's a mistake to let these quiet, inoffensive guys fool you when you're dealing with
murder," he said. "I was up with the F.B.I. for a spell.

Sort of goin' to class. Learned some things, most of them routine. Did some reading. It ain't only in books that a guy you'd never expect it of turns out to be a killer. Guys like Stinson. Quiet, hard workers, married mostly. Churchgoers. Teach in Sunday School. Never in trouble but all the time things building up inside them, or maybe just one thing building up. Then it happens. Quick. No planning generally, just the right time and the right opportunity."

"Have you talked to Stinson?"

"This morning. For two solid hours. Think I scared him a bit, too. He had the opportunity and the motive. Look at it this way. He goes along for three years, working hard to earn an interest in this motel. He's doing fine when along comes a guy by the name of Tyler and throws a wrench in the gearbox. Gannon blows his top. Says he'll mortgage the place and cut down the profits. Wants the books in order. Okay, now who knows if the books are going to be in order or not, or if there's a shortage?"

He went on without waiting for an answer. "One day Stinson's working along with only an interest in the profits of a place that's going to be mortgaged; the next he's the outright owner of twenty-five per cent of the property."

"Get back to those capsules," Dave said. "Did Stinson know Liza Drake well enough to pay her or force her into doping my drink so Gannon would be alone?"

"I don't think he knew her hardly at all. Wouldn't have to. The point is Stinson's at the motel working and he sees Gannon come home alone. First time he's been alone. All Stinson needs is five minutes. He don't care *why* Gannon's alone; he only knows here's his chance."

"Did you tell him what Mrs. Craft said?"

"Certainly I told him. That's when he started to scare."

"What did he say?"

"Denied it. Said Mrs. Craft was mistaken. Admitted he was outside about that time but said he was just out for a smoke and to look around. Wasn't going any place in particular."

"What do you think?"

"I think he's lying. If it was anybody but Mrs. Craft that saw him—a defense attorney could prove she was a busybody like you say and probably discredit her testimony—I might decide to hold him."

Dave made up his mind then. Experience had shown him that it was pretty silly to hold out on Vaughn. His own personal feelings no longer mattered and he accepted the fact that it was his job to help, no matter who got hurt in the process.

"I have a little something on Stinson that may help," he said.

"That," said Vaughn, with mild irony, "would be a novelty, coming from you."

Dave grinned to show he took no offense but his voice was serious, his words crisp and to the point.

"This isn't gossip," he said. "This you can prove, or disprove."

"I'm listening. Skip the prologue."

"I can't, not all of it. I have to tell you that Stinson was looking for a chance to go in business for himself."

"Who said so?"

"He did," Dave said and told of his earlier talk with the motel manager. "So yesterday afternoon I took a trip down to Eaton. I talked to the owner of the motel that Stinson was interested in."

"Wait a minute!" Vaughn sat up and reached for a pencil. "A man by the name of Greer, at the Villa Greer? Okay."

Dave told as much as he could remember of that conversation. He paused, leaning forward in his chair now, measuring his words.

"Stinson called Greer the night of the murder and asked if Greer would accept option money on the motel."

"Hold it!" Vaughn said when Dave started to continue. He waited three seconds and then, his manner at

once cold and businesslike, he said: "Now give it to me.
Take your time and get it right. Just like you remember
it."

He listened intently, no longer looking at Dave but
at the sheet of paper on his desk. From time to time he
made a note. When Dave finished he picked up the
sheet.

"Let's see if I got this straight. Stinson had been down
to see Greer. Came down last week again. The night of
the murder he phoned to ask if Greer would give him
a sixty-day option for a thousand dollars. Was supposed
to put the check in the mail yesterday. You don't know
what time it was Stinson made that call. All Greer said
was that it was late."

He put the paper down when Dave nodded and a
smile that was more satisfied than humorous grew in the
corners of his dark eyes.

"Okay," he said. "Now we're starting to move. When
we find out what time that call was made we may be in
business. If he made it after my investigation he's just
an eager damn fool who was so wrapped up with the
thought of having his own business that he couldn't
wait until morning. If he made that call *before* my investigation—"

He cut the thought short and stood up, a new brisk-
ness in his normally casual manner. "We'll check Mr.
Greer," he said. "Then, later this afternoon, I'll have
another try at Stinson. If he's our boy he'll crack. That
I will personally guarantee."

It was a quarter of twelve when Dave returned to
Seabeach and by the time he had parked the car Betty
Nelson had come out of the Coffee Shop and was walk-
ing his way. He went to meet her, aware that she was
hurrying and knowing something was bothering her.
As she spoke he knew why.

"Mrs. Craft," she said.

"Oh-oh. Last night?"

"No. Something else that happened this morning."

"What?"

"She wouldn't tell me. She wants to talk to you. . . . Now don't be like that," she added when Dave sighed loudly. "It might be important."

"If it is she'll tell Vaughn anyway so why not tell him now?"

Betty took him firmly by the arm and led him to Mrs. Craft's unit. The occupant awaited them. She bowed them into her room and asked them to be seated. She was wearing the same plain blue dress Dave had seen the other day and when she sat down she folded her hands in her lap. A twist of her mouth settled her upper plate in its proper place and then she was ready.

"I've always made it a point," she said, her glance fastened on her folded hands, "to mind my own business."

Oh, sure, Dave thought.

"I don't want you to think I'm just a meddlesome old busybody because I can assure you it is not true. But when murder has been done I think we all should help, in our own small ways, to bring the guilty to justice."

She looked up to see if her audience was in agreement, and apparently was reassured by the nods she received.

"She came just after eleven this morning," she said.

"Who?" Dave said.

"That hussy from down the road, that singer. . . . Now these walls"—she gave a flip of her fingers—"are not soundproof. They never are in any motel I've ever been in. You hear things. Even if they were soundproof you'd hear things. You couldn't help it with the windows open the way they usually are. Cars coming and going, children shouting, radios playing. It's a wonder a body can sleep at all."

She tightened her mouth as the thought came to her that she was digressing. She tried again.

"Mr. Tyler," she said, "has the next apartment. She came to see him. I was in my bathroom washing out some—some things. The windows were open."

"So you heard what they said."

Mrs. Craft drew herself erect in the chair, her gaze frosty. "Mr. Barnum," she said, with calculated severity, "I have just told you I do not eavesdrop. I just happened to—"

Dave cut her off. He said he was sorry. "What I meant was, you just happened to hear a word here and there that gave you the gist of the conversation."

"Exactly."

"And what was it about?"

"Blackmail!"

Mrs. Craft waited, her lips working on the upper plate. Dave looked at Betty and she cautioned him with her glance.

"Blackmail?" he parroted, not believing it but still interested in what was to follow.

"Blackmail," Mrs. Craft repeated.

"Who was doing it?"

"He was. Mr. Tyler."

"What did he want, money?"

"I gathered as much."

Dave found his interest mounting in spite of himself because here, for the first time, was the suggestion that Tyler and Liza Drake had known each other in the past. Either that or—

He cleared his throat. He said he understood that since Mrs. Craft was not listening she could not have heard much of what was said, but perhaps she could give him her general impression. She said she would be glad to, and what she had to say indicated that she had been listening very hard indeed.

"They were quarreling," she said. "At times their voices were raised."

"Mr. Tyler wanted money," Dave prompted.

"Help is the word he used. Financial help. Enough, he said, to tide him over until he could collect something on his share of the motel."

"And what did she say?"

"At first she said no and he said, 'How would you like

to go back to the Coast?' " She paused to make a deprecating gesture. "Of course I was busy. I could only get
a snatch of conversation now and then."

Dave said he understood. "Was anything more said
about the Coast?"

"He said something about dropping a word."

"Dropping a word?"

"Back on the Coast. Something like, 'If I dropped a
word back on the Coast it could be awkward for you,
couldn't it?' He said, 'Call it a loan. You do me a favor
and I'll do you one.' Something like that."

Mrs. Craft had very little to add but what she had
already said had Dave thinking hard. For it seemed now
that if Frank Tyler knew Liza Drake in connection with
something on the Coast, he had probably known her the
night John Gannon was murdered. It was almost a cer-
tainty that Tyler had seen Liza at the Club 80. And if
he knew enough, or thought he did, to extort money out
of Liza, he might well know enough to force her to use
her sleeping capsules on his, Dave's, drink.

"Did she give him the money?" he asked.

"I don't know. The first thing I knew the door
slammed and she was gone." She hesitated, fixing him
with her gaze. "What I wanted to know is, what should
I do? Do you think it would be wise for me to tell Captain Vaughn?"

Dave stood up. He was glad he had come. He had an
idea that most of what he had heard was true and while
he appreciated the information, he was at the same time
faintly disgusted by the methods used to get it.

"Why don't you do what you did before, Mrs. Craft?"

"I beg your pardon?"

"You told me about Stinson and then you told
Vaughn. Why shouldn't you tell him this?"

Mrs. Craft did not like the reply. Her pinched expression indicated that she classed it as impertinent. At
the door Dave gave her a thin smile.

"You could think it over," he said. "If you decide

you'd rather not tell the captain I could do it for you, if you like."

Mrs. Craft made no reply. Dave held the door for Betty and followed her out of the room.

14

BETTY HAD to rush back to the Coffee Shop and Dave wanted a swim before lunch, but there was one thing he wanted to do first. He had thought of it last night too late to do any good, and now, a glance at his watch telling him it would be nine fifteen in California, he went back to the bungalow, turned to the telephone, and asked for the long-distance operator.

"A person-to-person call," he said, "to Los Angeles. Mr. Jeffrey Harding." He spelled the name and gave the address, and ten minutes later he was talking to a man who had been his classmate at law school.

"I want you to check a will for me, Jeff," he said when the amenities were finished. "Got a pencil? . . . Okay. An Albert L. Colby. Died about six months ago, so the will should be a matter of record. . . . I'm not sure but it could be Los Angeles, Beverly Hills, or maybe Santa Monica."

He laughed at his friend's protest. "Sure, I know it's a lot of territory, but do the best you can. . . . Sure. . . . I'd like to know the will's provisions, the amount of the estate, who inherits. I think the firm handling the estate is Leeman & Vance. I can't give you the address but it should be in the Beverly Hills directory. . . . Good boy. Call me here between seven and eight, your time," he said, and gave his number. . . .

. Carl Workman and the Widow Collins had the beach to themselves and when Workman spotted Dave he beckoned.

"Park it, son," he said. "This is Mrs. Collins—Mr. Barnum. Thelma—Dave."

Thelma wore dark glasses that all but covered her penciled brows, so Dave could not tell much about her eyes or what she was thinking. He revised his opinion about her thinness as he sat down, for he saw now that there was enough roundness here and there to warrant the word *slender*. But he had been right about her age. Small lines had started to work along the corners of the mouth and eyes, and in the neck. Her face was oily with lotion but her skin was pale, and her slightly accented voice seemed more affected than cultured when she acknowledged the introduction.

"Thelma's been over around St. Petersburg," Workman said, "and she's having a look around this coast." He grinned at her and said: "She's decided to stay here a few days."

"I like it," she said, a faint huskiness in her languid voice. "This beach is quite marvelous."

She opened an expensive-looking straw bag and took out a leather cigarette case and a gold lighter. Workman took the lighter from her when she offered the case to Dave. She put a cork-tipped cigarette between her painted lips when Dave refused and held her face up so Workman could give her a light.

She chatted pleasantly on about this and that and Dave answered as pleasantly when an answer was necessary, the thought coming to him that somehow the woman reminded him of Liza. They could not have been more opposite in looks and figure and yet the idea remained they had much in common. He could not say why; he only knew that to him they seemed like the same type of woman, though exactly what that type was he did not know.

She came up on her knees when she flipped her cigarette away. She said she mustn't get too much sun at first. She brushed sand from her fingertips and fitted her cap with care around her auburn curls. When she removed her glasses Dave saw that her eyes were green; her glance, as she smiled at him, was bold and secretly speculating.

"Are you coming in?" she asked.

"In a minute," Workman said. "You go ahead."

She walked away, hips swinging and shoulders high. For a moment Workman seemed to watch her with approval and then his eyes sobered and he looked at Dave.

"How'd you make out?"

"About what?"

"With Vaughn. You said you had a date."

Dave considered the matter thoroughly before he replied. He had not talked to Workman before and was not sure that Vaughn would want him to go into the information he had about Stinson. On the other hand Workman had impressed him as a very capable guy. He had been a policeman himself; he was also under some suspicion. With the idea that it might be worth while to get Workman's reaction on certain things, he said that Vaughn was beginning to think that Stinson might be guilty.

"Me too," Workman said.

"Why?"

"Nothing in particular. It's just that I'm leery of these quiet, harmless-looking guys. They blow up all of a sudden. Stinson knew about the mortgage and he was here. If he made up his mind to do the job it would have been a cinch. *Was* a cinch—because up to now he's gotten away with it."

Dave listened to certain other remarks in the same vein, none of them new. He waited until Workman had finished before he changed the subject, reconsidering now an earlier decision.

"Who besides Resnik," he said, "would want to kill Betty?"

"Betty?" Workman gave him a hard bright stare. "Are you kidding?"

"I wish I thought so."

"When?"

"Last night on her way back from Boothville."

Then he told the story as he knew it, glancing covertly at the other from time to time. Workman did not seem to be aware of the inspection. He was staring seaward, his tanned face somber, his narrowed gaze bleak.

"You tell Vaughn?" he asked finally. "What did he say?"

"He said he hadn't been able to find out a thing."

"He'd need some luck on a caper like that. Probably a stolen car."

"Or a rented one. Resnik could arrange a thing like that."

"Resnik could if he had to." He gave Dave a moment of quick inspection. "You figure Resnik slugged you?"

"Yes."

"Ever figure that even if he did it wouldn't prove he killed Gannon? That shooting could have happened before."

Dave said it had occurred to him.

"I think you have to look at it this way," Workman said, deliberate now. "If Resnik shot Gannon he'd probably try a stunt like that with a car. If he did, and he failed last night, he'll try again. If he didn't kill Gannon, that's something else."

"If it wasn't Resnik, who was it?"

"There," said Workman, "you've got me." He might have said something more because deep down his amber eyes were disturbed. But just then Thelma called to him.

He looked at her standing thigh deep in the breaking surf. He said: "Nuts!" impatiently but he waved back at her and stood up. He looked down at Dave.

"I'll see you," he said. "Keep your eye on Betty, Barnum. We wouldn't want anything to happen to her. And it could, you know. It just possibly could."

Dave watched the tanned, muscular figure lope down toward the water. He considered what had been said and out of it all he had but one impression: Workman was disturbed. It showed in little ways that defied analysis but the impression remained.

It was one thirty before Dave was ready for lunch and when he realized he still had a half hour before the Coffee Shop would close he walked along the drive behind the units until he came to Stinson's stall.

The car was a two-year-old, two-door sedan, gray, the finish still quite good. Dave examined it from behind while he visualized the angle of contact a car would make in forcing another off the road.

"The right rear fender," he said, half aloud. "Or maybe that side of the bumper."

He moved a foot or so to his right and then he saw the scratch. It was a dent really, not deep, but there was a brightness of metal which suggested it had been put there not too long ago. It was well down near the rear of the flaring fin of the mudguard, just in front of the bumper. He stared at it, his interest quickening, and leaned close.

"Take it easy," he said to himself. "Don't get excited. You don't know if that dent was made yesterday, the day before, or five days ago."

He examined the surface to see if he could find any signs of a different color paint but detected nothing that helped him any. He was aware that the right sort of spectroscopic analysis might disclose something of value but there was certainly no clue that he could see with the naked eye. He backed away, the excitement still working on him. He examined the left rear fender.

There was a dent there too, though not in the same place and not so new looking. He moved toward the front and found a scratch on the left front fender and there was a scrape of paint, not gray, on the outer curve of the bumper which spoke of another near accident.

He moved back into the open, the excitement oozing away as common sense began to assert itself. The more he thought about it the more he realized that most cars nowadays had dents or scratches somewhere on them. And yet there was a stubbornness working on him too that made him continue his survey, bringing him now to the next stall and the small sedan which occupied it.

It was a current model with Florida plates, dusty but new looking underneath. The rear bumper had a dent in it. There was a scrape on the right rear fender that extended for a foot or more but was not deep enough to show the metal underneath. There was a scratch on the door panel.

He stuck his head in the lowered window on impulse, wondering who the car belonged to, and on the dash he saw a small metal plate which proclaimed the owner as a Drive-Urself establishment with a Tampa address.

"The Widow Collins," he muttered and backed away.

He glanced along the line of car-ports, empty now in the middle of the day. Betty's was on the other side and he intended to look that one over too before he finished, though by now he was ready to admit that his knowledge of such matters was not sufficiently expert to do much good.

Stopping again opposite Stinson's car, he stooped down to examine once more the dent he had first noticed. He was standing that way when he realized someone had come up beside him unnoticed.

"Looking for something?" George Stinson said, pleasantly enough.

Dave flushed and felt embarrassed. Stinson's pink face held a half-smile, and behind the spectacles his light-blue eyes were curious but not annoyed. Dave gave him a moment of thoughtful regard and, because the strain had been working on him for quite a while, he saw the other not as a polite and inoffensive man who had always been pleasant to everyone but as a possible murderer. He himself was by nature courteous and considerate of the feelings of others. Now, however, he answered directly, deciding to play it on the nose.

"I was wondering when you got that dent."

Stinson bent down to see what Dave meant. He shook his head and made a noise in his throat that sounded like a small chuckle.

"I don't know," he said. "I didn't even know it was there."

"Someone back into you while you were parked?"

Stinson's smile went away. "I told you," he said stiffly, "it's the first I've seen it."

"Were you on the road last night?"

"When?"

"Any time."

"Why?"

"Because someone tried to force Betty down a bank last night on her way back from Boothville." He went on, his tone level and distinct, seeing the stiffness grow in Stinson's face as the color left it but keeping on until he had finished.

"You're suggesting it might be me," Stinson said, his voice shaking.

"That dent's in the right spot. I was just wondering."

Stinson's eyes flared and the temper that Dave had wondered about came to the surface. He took a small step forward.

"Why, damn you, Barnum! I've got a good notion to—" He did not finish the sentence but he looked mad enough to do whatever it was he had in mind. "Betty!" he said. "You miserable young sneak! What the hell do you mean by accusing me?"

He took another step, his lips quivering as he fought to control them. "Get away from that car and stay away from it. If you're so damn sure of yourself why don't you go to the police?"

Dave backed up a step without realizing it, so savage were the manager's words. The fury of it surprised him not only because the reaction seemed out of proportion to the provocation, but because it suggested the reaction of a man already emotionally disturbed.

"I have," he said and then, not meaning to but stung by Stinson's manner, the rest of it slipped out.

"I also went to Eaton yesterday afternoon," he said, "and talked to Ed Greer about that motel you're going to buy, that option you were in such a hurry to get."

He knew it was not his business to be accusing Stinson, not his business at all. It was Vaughn's job and

Vaughn would know how to handle it. He knew that, as he spoke and saw Stinson's bespectacled face compose itself in stiffness, its color gone, the eyes stricken.

"Vaughn's checking," he said. "He'll be around to—"

He broke abruptly because he was talking to himself. Stinson had turned on his heel and now he was walking rapidly away and Dave watched him, feeling ashamed not so much at his outburst as at his own lack of self-control. What, he asked himself, was getting into him? Why should he be so nerved-up and jumpy and uncertain?

15

DAVE AND Betty went to the beach that afternoon shortly after three. Far to the right Frank Tyler lay on his back sunning himself. Fifty feet away and somewhat nearer the water Carl Workman was stretched out on his stomach, a towel covering part of his head. To the left, in isolated splendor, Mrs. Craft was asleep under her umbrella.

They spread their beach towels and got cigarettes going and stretched out on their stomachs to improve their tans. Then, because they had never been alone like this since that first day on the beach, they began to talk about themselves as is the custom with couples in love.

What they had to say was neither new nor original, for they spoke of likes and dislikes and were happily surprised to discover that, along with millions of others, they shared a mutual fondness for sea food, with particular emphasis on oysters and lobster, medium rare steaks, green salads, and blueberry pie. Music, they decided, was a must, especially "Dixie" when the mood was right. Bach, Beethoven, and the longhairs were absolutely essential, but between them and "Dixie" there was not too much to excite them. Piano players and records, yes. Chopin and Tatum, Horowitz and Chittison.

It was all good fun and it took them quite a while to cover the subject thoroughly. Finally, her mood suddenly more thoughtful, Betty asked what Dave would do now. He had leaned up on one elbow to watch her better and he was examining the way her sun-bleached brown hair grew along the side of her head above the ear, the spacing of the freckles on the bridge of her small cute nose. He said what did she mean, what was he going to do?

"Well—you'll be sort of rich now, won't you?"

He chuckled at her frown. He said he didn't think so. He said he didn't know if the Club 80 property was free and clear or not. He didn't know anything about Gannon's debts or what the taxes and estate expenses would be.

"Of course I'll have something," he said. "Maybe more than I ever expected to have at one time. But I can't see how it will make much difference. Maybe I'll drive a Pontiac or a Buick instead of a Ford, and I can have a nicer apartment. But other than that—"

He let the sentence hang as his mind went on. "I'm a lawyer," he said, his voice slow with thought. "I'm with a fine firm and if I keep my eye on the ball I should do all right. Money? I figure if you get money you can lose it too. Bad investments, speculation, one thing or another. The only real security a man has is within himself. If I'm a good lawyer and I work at my trade I'll have a knowledge and experience and some sort of success that no one can take away from me, whether I've got money in the bank or not."

It was quite a speech and he realized how it might sound. He was about to say something to counteract it, when he saw a gleam in Betty's eyes that stopped him. He did not know what it was because he had never seen it before. He only knew that the hazel eyes were softly misty, that what he saw way down deep quickened his pulse and was very wonderful to behold.

She could not have known about the look but she

must have known how she felt. Perhaps she realized
she was exposing some secrets of her own because in
the next instant she smiled brightly and glanced over
at Mrs. Craft.

"Do you think she's asleep?"

"No."

"Why?"

"Because there are people on the beach and things to
see."

"Like what?"

"Like us. If you think she's bored I could give her
something to think about."

She considered this with open eyes. "Oh?"

"If I sat up and kissed you—"

He sat up.

She sat up.

Her eyes said she approved but her voice and manner were mockingly horrified.

"You wouldn't dare."

He laughed aloud. Over under the umbrella Mrs.
Craft stirred. "Come on," he said, "let's get wet." He
offered a hand and pulled her to her feet and they
headed for the lines of curling surf.

The afternoon had nearly gone when Dave had finished dressing. He was glad about that because he had
nothing to do except eat and wait around for a telephone call from California that would not come until
ten o'clock.

At six o'clock he remembered about the news. The
radio was still tuned to station WTCX so he snapped
it on and listened absently. Then he sat by the front
window to watch the activity outside, for this was the
time of day the tourists began to stop for the night and
the routine always fascinated him. It gave his imagination something to do as he speculated about these
people who came so swiftly and were as swiftly gone
when morning came.

A car would pull in—mostly northbound cars at this

time of year—and either the man or the woman would get out, a little stiffly usually, and stumble toward the office door. There would be a minute or so of preliminary decision made at the desk and then the man or woman would come out and get back into the car.

This, to the observer, was the crucial moment. Either the car would whip back onto the highway in search of other quarters or turn slowly into the drive. At the same time George Stinson or Mrs. Leland, who lived down the road and acted as a sort of managerial assistant, would come out, key in hand, and move along the lawn to a vacant unit while the car nosed into the proper port. Then both the man and woman would appear to inspect the premises. Usually that was the end of it and Mrs. Leland—it was Mrs. Leland who was doing the honors tonight—would scurry back to await the next car. Some time later the NO VACANCY sign was usually flashed on and that was the end of the performance for the day.

Dave snapped off the radio when the news was finished. He started toward the kitchen to make his nightly cocktail and then he turned back, his dark-blue eyes focused in thought and a new narrowness growing in them as his frown came.

He turned again, more slowly this time, and went into the kitchen. He made his drink at the sink, a dry martini which he stirred in a beer glass and then poured into a generous-sized cocktail glass. Forgoing the olive because there were none, he stood at the sink and drank it while distance grew in his gaze. Finally, his drink finished, he went to the Coffee Shop and had his dinner before the place became too crowded with transients.

He was back in his chair by the window at twenty minutes after seven and he sat there in the gathering darkness, exploring the unlit, silent place of his mind and watching the activity outside: the later arrivals who had reservations and came to be shown their quarters, the almost unfailing trip, pitcher in hand, to the ice-

house, a squarish, roofed structure resembling a well
house into which was nightly dumped a washtub full of
ice cubes. Then there was the stroll to the Coffee Shop,
the children playing on the lawn until their parents
called them in. Finally the NO VACANCY sign flashed on
and quiet came. It was then that he saw the two men
walk up to Frank Tyler's unit and knock at the door.

He had not noticed the car and decided it had been
parked along the highway since the men approached
from the front. It was not quite dark, and while the distance was too great to reveal much about their faces,
something about the way they walked held Dave's
attention.

They wore dark suits and no hats. They kept step as
they approached, marching rather than walking, looking
neither to the right or left, one about average size, the
other somewhat taller and broader. The tall one did
the knocking. When the door opened he stepped inside
immediately, followed by his companion.

Without realizing it Dave had leaned forward in his
chair; now he walked to his door and peered through
the screen. Something, he did not know what, told him
instinctively that these were not ordinary visitors intent
on a social call. A half minute later, when the light went
out in Tyler's place and the trio appeared, he was sure
of it.

They started marching again. Tyler was out of step,
but they were marching just the same, the actor in the
middle and slightly in advance. When they started toward the Coffee Shop and the road, Dave slipped out
the door and climbed into the sedan. Just what he expected to learn he was not sure, but his curiosity was a
driving force now as he backed out of the car-port and
rolled along behind the next bungalow and the units on
that side.

As he approached the highway he saw a car parked
on the opposite side of the road and headed for the
Club 80. The door on the driver's side was just closing
and when the car angled into the road he picked a hole

in the oncoming traffic and followed along with only one car separating him from the one he was watching.

They passed the club without slowing down and somehow this surprised Dave. A few minutes later he could see the lights of Vantine up ahead; just then the car directly in front of him passed the first one, and now he saw the automatic signaling device winking on the left rear fender.

There was a street here that led to the beach, well built up with courts and small apartment houses and some efficiency units. Not wanting to follow too closely, Dave reduced his speed and when he saw the stoplights flash red on the car ahead he cut his own lights and pulled quickly into the curb.

The other car had stopped about a hundred yards away in front of a two-story, rectangular building on the left-hand side of the street. When he saw the trio start up the walk, he crossed to the opposite side and hurried toward the beach. Only then did he realize that the building had no front entrance but actually faced a strip of lawn extending from front to rear. For that reason the entrances to the various units came from that side, the lower doors opening from the walk while those above were reached by separate railed-in stairs and landings, with small sun decks adjacent to each landing.

Luckily the trio's goal was the last apartment, otherwise Dave might not have known where they went. As it was he saw them climbing the rearmost flight of stairs, and the moment they disappeared he hurried along the walk.

Looking up as he reached the stairs he saw that the windows and the glass door were of louver construction which meant that if the angles of opening were right he would not be able to see inside the room, but neither would anyone be able to look out. So he went up the steps on tiptoe, keeping close to the building, hearing voices now but unable to understand what was being said until he reached the landing. The louvers in the door were of opaque glass and had been cranked down-

ward so he could not see in, but he knew now that this
was Resnik's apartment, for it was Resnik who was doing the talking.

Resnik never talked loud but he talked distinctly.
What Dave did not realize until very nearly too late
was that the interview was almost over.

Tyler had not been inside more than two minutes.
There must have been some preliminary explanation or
discussion, but now there was no other voice but Resnik's as he said:

"Let's put it this way, Tyler. This is just a warning.
There doesn't have to be any trouble. It's up to you.
Open your mouth about Liza and I'll take care of you.
She's a long way from the Coast and she wants to keep
it that way. I understand you're an actor."

There was a moment of silence but no answer. Resnik
said: "Sort of a pretty one too, hunh? Well, get this.
You get out of line with Liza and you'll have trouble
getting work. You may do all right on radio but you'll
never be on television, except maybe as Dracula. Is that
clear?"

The reply was mumbled and indistinct but apparently
Resnik accepted it as an affirmative.

"Be smart, Tyler," he said. "Stay healthy. . . . All
right. Take him back home."

With that the interview was over and there was a
sound of movement behind the louvered door and
Dave was caught flat-footed. He was not scared but
neither did he want to be caught outside just then. As
he stiffened and glanced down at the ground he
heard the latch click. What saved him was the sun
deck.

The railing was no more than two feet high and he
stepped over it silently and flattened himself against
the wall, breath held and head turned.

He heard the door open, the sound of feet. Light cut
the darkness and spread across the landing and the lawn
below. Then the door closed and the steps were going
down. He stood as he was, stretched tall and immobile.

He waited until he heard the car door slam. He relaxed and waited a minute or so longer. Then he stepped back on the landing and knocked at the door.

It was the first time Dave ever saw Resnik register surprise. In that first instant when he recognized his caller his gambler's eyes could not quite cope with the discovery. They opened as his jaw sagged, working into a scowl before he could steady them again. After that things were normal and there was no surprise in his voice.

"Come in," he said. And when he had closed the door: "Snooping?"

"Sort of. I followed Tyler."

Resnik had apparently been getting into his nightly uniform. He wore tropical-weight dress trousers, patent-leather pumps and a soft, pleated shirt open at the throat. Now he took a cigarette from a silver box. While he lit it Dave glanced round, recognizing the layout as what was commonly called an efficiency apartment and impressed with what he saw. The huge room was taste-fully furnished in the modern way, its pieces conserva-tively upholstered in neutral colors and comfortable looking. A glass-brick partition was topped by a com-position counter and separated a small dining table from the small but complete kitchen. Through a partly open door he could see a sizable dressing room with built-in chests and beyond that the bath. The oversized couch in the corner would, he knew, become an over-sized bed with the removal of its tailored cover.

"Why?"

Resnik was watching him over the still burning match.

"I saw those two come for Tyler. They looked like hoods."

Resnik's neat little mustache curved in a smile. "They wouldn't like to hear you say that."

"I was curious."

Resnik examined the end of his cigarette, head slightly bent. He let his glance come up without mov-ing his head.

"Hear anything?"

"Part of it."

"You do all right for an amateur. You ought to stay that way. . . . What do you think now?" he said after a moment.

"Tyler tried to make a touch from Liza this morning," Dave said. "Maybe polite blackmail. She told you and you threw a scare into Tyler to keep him quiet." He grinned but not with his eyes. "I imagine he was impressed. I know I would have been."

Resnik nodded and it was no longer possible to tell what he was thinking, so inscrutable was his gaze.

"Anything else?"

"A little," Dave said. "It'll take a while. I've told the story before but not to you."

With that he sat down and told about the empty sleeping capsules. He said he was convinced Liza was involved but he was not sure just how.

"She'd do a thing like that for you because she loves you," he said. "She could have done it for Gannon because it might appeal to his sense of humor as a very good gag. Now I'm wondering if she might have done it for Tyler."

Resnik sat down. He put his head back and stared at the ceiling. When he spoke Dave thought the voice sounded concerned.

"I hadn't heard about the Mickey," he said. "I'm not sure I believe it. I'll ask her but I doubt if she'd pull a stunt like that for Tyler."

"He tried to blackmail her. He's got some hold on her."

"Some. A matter of being a witness. There are some who want her to testify and others who don't. She's in the middle. I happen to be in love with her. We're going to be married as soon as the new lease is signed and I can be sure I'm in business for another three years."

"She told me."

"I wouldn't want her to get mixed up in anything,"

Resnik said as though he had not heard, "because of some jerk like Tyler."

"Ask her about the capsules," Dave said. "If she didn't do it for Tyler, maybe she did it for you."

"Maybe she didn't do it at all." Resnik stood up and moved into the dressing room. He turned on the overhead light and began to put on his black tie, his chin high as he buttoned the shirt. "You sort of like me for the shooting, don't you?"

"I talked to Willie Shear."

Resnik made his bow and tugged at the ends. "You get around."

"He told me how it was with you and Gannon." Dave stood up. "All I know," he said, seeing no harm in saying what he thought, "is that unless the agreement can be broken—which I doubt—you're sitting pretty. With Gannon alive you'd be out on the street with your furniture in about three more days."

Resnik wrapped a cummerbund about his slim waist. When he had it adjusted to his satisfaction he moved back into the room. He looked very neat, very smooth. He did not have Willie Shear's quality or standing but then he was some years younger than Willie and he was on his way up. He moved toward Dave, feeling again for the ends of his tie and tightening the bow gently, and he apparently did not like what Dave had just said. The angles of his jaw were ridged; there were unpleasant glints in his gambler's eyes.

"You're a pretty smart lad, Barnum," he said. "Just stay smart. Don't start playing detective." He rose and balanced his weight on his toes. "That witness business about Liza. Don't let it get around unless you want trouble."

"You're in love with her," Dave said. "You wouldn't want anything to happen to her."

"Now you've got it."

"Well, I'm in love with Betty Nelson. I wouldn't want anything to happen to her either, but I'm a little worried."

"Betty? What could happen to her?"

"Last night something almost did," Dave said and then, though he had wearied of the telling, he gave another account to Resnik, who stood motionless, his pale face impassive, his gaze inscrutable.

Dave did not wait for any reaction or comment. When he had finished his story he turned and left the room.

16

DAVE BARNUM was not sure just what time it was when he swung the sedan into the car-port beside the darkened bungalow. He was still thinking of his encounter with Resnik and he paid no attention to the car that was parked a short distance ahead until its lights snapped on and he heard the door open. Then he saw the buggy-whip antenna, the siren, the oversized spotlight.

Oh-oh, he thought, when he saw the uniformed officer move toward him.

"Barnum?"

"Yes," Dave said.

"Captain Vaughn wants to see you." The officer was close now, a well-built young man wearing a cartridge belt and a holstered revolver. "Been waiting for you."

"Long?"

"Not very. You can ride with me."

Dave started to walk along with the policeman, curious and oddly disturbed.

"What's he want to see me about?"

"He'll tell you."

They went a few steps farther and then Dave remembered the telephone call he hoped to get around ten o'clock. At the car door he glanced at his watch in the reflected light and saw that it was a minute or two after nine.

"Do you think we'll be long?" he asked.

The officer continued in the same uncommunicative vein. He said he couldn't say. He slid in behind the wheel and kicked the starter and then they were riding the gravel behind the right-hand units and turning left into the highway with a touch of the siren.

They did not go very far. The red police light flashed a warning to motorists in both directions and then, a second or so after he had shifted into high, the officer swung diagonally across the wrong side of the road and hit his brakes.

Across on the right-hand side of the highway was a fruit stand, closed now, its front shuttered. Almost opposite this was a narrow road leading to the beach. The headlights picked out the sign by the side of it and Dave read it before they pulled past and slid to a stop.

DEAD END. NO ENTRY.

Dave had never noticed the sign before but he had seen the road which was black topped and overgrown with shrubs and creepers at the shoulders. What he learned presently was that it at one time led to one end of the public beach. There was a turn-around at the end on the small bluff overlooking this but a storm two years ago had undercut it, crumbling the foundation and rendering it useless. The same storm had washed away the sand at this particular point so that now the rocks were exposed well out into the water, rendering the bathing hazardous and forming a sort of barrier between the public beach and the one which joined that at the motel. The beach here was perfectly passable; it was just that no one ever swam there.

Now, as they got out of the car, Dave saw the second policeman and he stood at one side while the two men exchanged words. The one who had been waiting stepped into the car and Dave's companion started off on foot.

"Down this way, Mr. Barnum," he said. "It's not very far."

Dave saw the lights as he started down the road. He could not tell what they were but they looked like car headlights and as he drew closer he realized that there were three cars in all, standing in line with no way out except to back. The first was a sedan with a doctor's shield above the license plate. The next, he saw even before they had reached the sedan, was an ambulance. There was a gap just beyond it where some men had gathered on the road and then there was this gray Chevrolet sedan, its outlines stark and vivid in the glare of the headlights behind it.

Until now Dave had not known quite what to expect. He understood in the beginning that whatever the occasion it was important. He knew it was urgent or he would not have been sent for.

A growing apprehension and uneasiness had become harder to control as the minutes passed. He had been conditioned to expect almost anything but he could not keep out the fear that had started to gnaw insidiously at his insides, a fear born of imagination that could think only of the accident that had nearly happened the night before, the inadmissible but ever-present thought that it might happen again.

For the last minute or so he had walked along on wooden legs, his mind closed against the possibility. His nerves tightened with each step he took and there was a spasmodic irregularity to his breathing. He was afraid to ask questions, afraid to think. He concentrated on one thought alone and kept repeating it silently over and over again. Not Betty, not Betty . . .

He made himself keep moving even when he saw the covered stretcher around which the men had gathered. He thought he recognized one as the doctor who had been at the bungalow the other night. He forced his glance upward. It was then that he really saw the gray sedan and only then did his mind find release and begin to function.

A moment later he was ashamed of the almost over-
whelming relief that swept through him and broke the
icy grip of all that terrifying tension. Like that the answer came to him. For he had spent some time inspecting that gray sedan and even now the dent on the right
rear fender stood out clearly in the bright glare of the
lights.

He began to sweat as he came to a stop, and his knees
started to tremble. He looked at the stretcher and then
away. He glanced from one face to the other until
Captain Vaughn emerged from the shadows and came
striding forward.

Vaughn spoke bluntly, his drawl gone and exasperation riding his words. "Where were you?" he demanded.

Dave started to answer and discovered he had to
swallow before he could speak. He ignored the question.

"Stinson?"

"Stinson. You want to look?"

"No."

"Come here." Vaughn took him by the arm and led
him alongside the gray sedan. He pointed inside. "We
found him behind the wheel about a half hour ago.
Some guy wanted to do a little night surf casting or
he'd been here till morning."

Dave looked through the window but he did not see
it. What he saw was George Stinson in his anger before
he went to lunch. He heard in fancy the things that
were said. He thought of his own suspicions and he remembered the Villa Greer and Stinson's ambition to
own it. They kept piling upon him, these thoughts, and
suddenly he felt sick. He had to back away quickly and
gulp and swallow fast. He stepped to the edge of the
bushes, head back and taking deep breaths.

Vaughn seemed to understand the reason for all this
and waited considerately for a few seconds. He pulled
out a pack of cigarettes and offered them.

"Want to try one?"

"Not now," Dave said. "I'm okay. It sort of hit me for
a moment. I was talking to him this morning."

"Let's try it again," Vaughn said. "Where were you?"

"Tonight?"

"Earlier. Say around three o'clock."

"On the beach."

"Alone?"

"With Betty Nelson."

"Um." Vaughn stood for a moment looking out over the ocean. He turned to look back at those behind the sedan, his dark weathered face squinting into the lights. Dave, trying to follow his gaze, saw that the stretcher was being lifted into the ambulance. Behind it the doctor's car was starting to back up. Just when he thought Vaughn had finished with him the captain said: "How long would you say you were with her?"

Dave said he wasn't sure but it was after four when they left. Vaughn nodded and gave him a moment of thoughtful inspection, his lips working silently. Dave looked at the sedan.

"Was he shot?" he asked.

"Once. Close up."

"Like Gannon."

"Only under the arm. Looks like I was wrong," Vaughn said. "Didn't think we'd ever have to worry about that gun. Thought the ocean was too close."

He took his straw hat off and rubbed his close-cropped hair. He put the hat back on.

"We've got no ballistics department in Vantine," he said. "Take us maybe a day to be sure but my guess is it's the same gun. We checked the first slug and shell. The experts seem to think it might be a Mauser. . . . When'd you last see Stinson?"

"Around a quarter of two," Dave said and tried to shut his mind against the memory.

"Doc seems to think it happened between three and five this afternoon. I guess it's just as well you have an alibi for part of that time."

He stopped as one of his men with a flashlight in his hand climbed the bank from the beach. Vaughn went to meet him and they talked for a minute in low tones.

Another man joined them and then the two began to sweep the sides of the road with their lights. Vaughn came back.

"Just for the record," he said, "we'll have a look at your bungalow. . . . Steve!"

The young officer who had brought Dave here emerged from the shadows.

"Take Mr. Barnum back to his bungalow," Vaughn said. "Go through everything. Anything that's locked, he'll unlock it for you. Keep him with you. Let him see what you're doing." He took the officer by the arm and turned him toward the highway.

"You're looking for a gun, or shells. Anything else that looks interesting you can tell me about when I get there." To Dave he said: "I'll be along. Wait there for me."

17

IT WAS hard for Dave Barnum to realize that he had been at the murder scene less than fifteen minutes. Yet it was only twenty minutes after nine when he walked into the bungalow, and for a little while he stopped worrying about his telephone call.

It took Vaughn's man, Steve, no more than ten minutes to go over the interior. He insisted that Dave accompany him when he went into the other apartment, but when it was all over he had found nothing that seemed important. Then, apparently having other orders that had been given him before, he told Dave to wait and left the place. About five minutes later Carl Workman came in.

He was clad in slacks and one of his short-sleeved shirts, but he had a necktie on and looked more dressy than usual. He had a cord jacket over one arm and he tossed this on the settee and dropped down beside it,

not saying anything until he'd stretched his legs out
wearily.

"They're searching my place," he said finally. "Told
'em I'd wait over here." He stared straight ahead, his
hard-jawed face somber, his amber gaze bleak. "I guess
you know what happened."

Dave nodded.

"Stinson," Workman said. "I always thought he might
have pulled the first job but I never figured he'd be
dumb enough to get himself killed. I understand it happened down that dead-end road."

Dave said he had been there and seen the car. He
told what he knew and Workman just sat there staring
straight ahead while a narrowness grew in his eyes.

"Would you have a drink in the joint?" he asked
abruptly.

Dave said yes and went into the kitchen to make
highballs. He put out two glasses and got some ice and
then, as he started to pour the whisky, the sight of it
revolted him and he made only one drink.

Workman gulped thirstily and said: "Ahh." He took
another swallow. "You talked to the captain. . . .
What's he think?"

"He didn't say and I didn't ask him. He said to wait
here."

"Stinson," Workman said again. "Makes you kind of
sick to your stomach."

Dave sat down and said nothing. He wished Vaughn
would hurry up and come in, and presently the wish
was granted. Vaughn came in with Steve. He looked at
Dave and then at Workman but said nothing. He took
off his hat and put it on top of the radio and then the
telephone rang.

Dave sat up, nerve ends tingling as he silently prayed
the call would not be for him. Not here, not now. It
wasn't. Vaughn answered, identified himself, listened,
spoke cryptically and hung up.

For the next fifteen minutes the routine was repeated
and the bungalow became a base of operations. Plain-

clothes men and uniformed officers came and went, entering through Dave's door and remaining on that side so that Vaughn talked to them there. What was said was never disclosed either to Dave or to Workman, who sat mute, inspecting his empty glass from time to time with an expression that suggested he wished he had a refill. Twice Vaughn went out for a few minutes and came back, but Steve was always there and during those intervals the bungalow was silent. Finally Vaughn pulled up a chair and sat down. Once again he looked from Workman to Dave and it seemed pretty obvious that his patience had worn thin.

Heretofore he had been investigating a murder, running down his leads as best he could and hoping for a break. Now he had a second death to cope with and the thought of failure was riding him hard and he could not help but think of the consequences. He was acting chief-of-police. There would be a day not too far distant when the title would be made permanent. That was how it had appeared up until two days ago. Now trouble was piling up on him and he had nothing to show for it, no progress to report.

For all of that his resentment was not directed at Workman or Dave. It showed in his face but he took his time and seemed to be selecting his words before he spoke. He still needed help and what he had to say concerned George Stinson, but it occurred to Dave that the captain was using them as a sounding board, wanting to express aloud the thoughts that had been building up in his mind so he could clarify them.

"How do you figure a guy like Stinson?" he said, expecting no answer. "Mrs. Craft was right. She saw him and he *was* coming here that first night. Either then or later he saw something. Maybe he heard the shot, maybe not. Maybe what he saw meant nothing to him until later."

He hesitated, his dark gaze exasperated and a bitterness in his voice that was still directed at the dead man.

"Would you ever figure a prissy little guy like him as

a blackmailer? As a killer, yes, with the proper provocation. But a blackmailer."

He stopped to curse, a frustrated sound. "What the hell did he want, money? He'd just inherited a quarter interest in this place. He had money in the bank."

Workman cleared his throat. "He forgot he was dealing with a killer."

"I threw a scare into him this morning," Vaughn said, as though he had not heard.

So did I, Dave thought, and said nothing about it.

"I knew then that he was mixed up in the thing some way. I wasn't sure he was my boy, but I could tell he was holding something back. I thought I'd give him a little more rope, give him a chance to think and then hit him hard this afternoon, haul him down, and book him if he wouldn't talk. I came for him a little after three. He was out."

"By that time," Workman said, "he must have already made his date."

"Sure," Vaughn said. "His last pitch. He was scared and the killer knew he could no longer be trusted. Drove down that road. A hell of a swell spot for the job. Hardly hear a shot inside the car like that. Somebody came up from the beach—"

"From the beach?" Workman sat up slowly and put his glass aside.

Vaughn nodded. When he spoke again some of the exasperation was gone so that his words became matter-of-fact rather than personal.

"We got a little break," he said. "We get 'em once in a while. . . . There's a little fruit stand nearly opposite that road," he said. "Family stand. They take turns at the counter."

Dave remembered. He had passed the stand daily. It offered oranges and tangerines in large and small baskets, and now and then grapefruit. QUALITY FRUITS, the sign said. SEND A BASKET HOME.

"This afternoon," Vaughn said, "business was slow. It's Grandpa's turn on the two-to-six shift so he sits there

in the shade and watches the cars go by. A little after
three he sees Stinson's sedan turn into the road. He
can't see down the road because of the angle but he sees
the car make the turn. The car never backs out."

He paused and Dave waited for the other essential
point to be made. Presently Vaughn made it.

"Nobody walks down that road either. If he had, the
old boy would have noticed because he's got nothing
else to do but notice things like that. No other car goes
in, none comes out, nobody shows at all."

"That makes it the beach," Workman said. He leaned
forward, the moisture along his widow's peak glistening
in the light. "The trouble is anybody could have walked
up from that public beach and—"

"Not anybody," Vaughn cut in. "Not without being
noticed by somebody, not with a gun. Because," he said,
"at this time of year there're not many transients using
that beach. Some regulars use it every day, old people
mostly. We'll find out who they are and check 'em. It
won't be any regulars because none of 'em are involved,
but the regulars notice the transients."

He put his palms on his kneecaps. "You take the kind
of trunks men wear nowadays and there's no place to
hide a gun, not even a little gun like this Mauser. A robe
or a towel would do it. Anybody walks toward that
rocky part of the beach with a robe would be noticed.
Same way with a towel because nobody would go in
swimming from that spot, so why a towel? . . . And
who," he asked, "says the guy had to come from the
public beach?"

He eyed Dave aslant, then focused on Workman, who
considered the question and then shrugged.

"This beach is just as close to that bluff as the public
one." Vaughn looked back at Dave. "You were here from
three to four or so. Who else that you know of?"

"Me," Workman said.

"When and how long?"

Workman eyed him resentfully and his mouth dipped
at one corner. His tanned face was set and the clipped,

hard inflection of his voice reminded Dave again that Workman had once been a policeman himself.

"I got to hand it to you," he said. "You get a big mark for trying."

"You think you're clean on this?"

"I know you think I'm not."

Vaughn smiled, a cold and humorless expression that made Dave glad the captain was not working on him. He spoke quietly and made as if to stand.

"You want to answer the question here or take a ride down to the station?"

"Who says I'm going to answer it at all?"

"You want to bet?"

Workman bunched his lips. He inhaled through his nose, the nostrils flaring as he studied Vaughn. Then he conceded the argument.

"I got to the beach before Dave and Betty. Frank Tyler was there when I got there. Part of the time I slept. They"—he glanced at Dave—"left before I did."

"Mrs. Craft was there too," Dave said.

"Ahh," said Vaughn. "Mrs. Craft."

He stood up and reached for his hat. It was a Leghorn type but an imitation and he gave a hard tug at the brim as he settled it on his head.

"You might hang around a bit longer," he said to Dave. "If you want to go to bed, okay. I've got to talk to Sam Resnik. I don't know if I'll be back or not. Probably not tonight."

To Workman he said nothing at all; he simply turned and walked out.

Workman rose after the door closed. He looked a little sheepish but his eyes were still resentful.

"I guess I played that one like a chump." He picked up his cord coat. "He made me sore," he said. "But he's a good man. I should've played it smarter."

When Dave made no move he went over to the door and then glanced at his strap watch. "Ten thirty," he said. "I guess that screws up the evening. Vaughn

didn't say so but if I don't stick around too he'll probably look me up and send the wagon."

Betty Nelson cried a little after Captain Vaughn had
gone. She had controlled herself pretty well at first
because the shock of what he had told her had left her
stunned and incapable of any deep feeling. In her mind
there was only disbelief and she had answered the questions in a monotone, hardly knowing what she said.
The captain had been gentle and considerate and he did
not stay long. He said he would not have to bother her
again that night and he would see that his men did not
disturb her.

Even now with the tears gone she could not make herself accept the fact of Stinson's death, and it was not just
because he had given her her first real job or that he
had been so patient and helpful in all his dealings with
her. She did not ask herself why he had been killed nor
did she speculate on who had done it; she simply sat
there, her mind a little sick and unable yet to associate
the man with the violence which had taken his life.

She was never sure how long she sat there. Once she
had started to go to the bungalow, wanting to know
about Dave, wanting to be with him for a little while.
But when she went to the door she could see the police
car out back and knew that he would have no time for
her. When she looked again his lights were out and
she did not know whether he had gone away with the
police or whether he was in bed. Wanting desperately to
talk to him for a little while, yet lacking somehow the
courage to bring herself to walk over there and knock
at the door, she sat there with the heat of the room closing in on her, feeling the dampness working on her
scalp and the stickiness of the skin beneath her clothes.

Finally, unable to bear it any longer, she stood up,
knowing what would help, what she really wanted to
do. For a fleeting instant, as she worked the zipper on
her cotton dress, a slight thrust of doubt passed through

her but she dismissed it and stepped out of the dress.

She had been swimming nightly for ten days or more and why, she asked herself, should this night be any different? No one would bother her, or even know she was gone, and besides the police were still here; at least one man who was still poking around in Stinson's apartment. She could see the lights and the moving shadow beyond the blinds.

She unsnapped her brassière and shrugged out of it. She peeled off her panties and her skin felt stickier than ever and there was no air to cool it even now. She pulled on her blue one-piece suit, took her robe from the closet, and found a towel. She did not bother with a bag but carried her cigarettes and matches in her hand. Then she was outside and walking swiftly toward the beach, wondering again about Dave as she passed between the bungalows.

Once past the bordering fringe and out on the sand, she turned toward the dune she usually chose, leaning back against it after she had spread her robe and feeling the welcome coolness of the night air against her hot, moist skin.

She lit a cigarette and stared seaward at the white line of breakers that came in with almost monotonous regularity. She could hear the crunch and boom as they broke, and the faint swish that followed as they swept across the firmly packed sand. She made another attempt to force her thoughts from George Stinson and this time they slid off on a tangent and she found a new cause for concern, this time a practical matter that involved her.

Who, she asked herself, was going to run the motel now that George was gone? Mrs. Leland could fill in when needed, just as she always did. The work and duties had been well organized and the rest of the help would do what they had to do. But George Stinson *was* the Seabeach Motel. What would Dave do? Who could he get, or would he have to close down temporarily?

Thus occupied she lost track of time. She lit another

cigarette. Once she thought she heard someone moving
on the sand and sat up quickly to scan the beach. The
sky was partly overcast but some light filtered through
to make odd-shaped shadowy objects of the other dunes.
But nothing moved and there was no sound but that of
the surf. When she turned to look back at the motel
there was only the sand and shadows, with here and
there a point of light showing beneath the silhouetted
palms.

The effort of looking, the fleeting thought that she
might not be alone, served to set in motion a strange
sense of uneasiness. After that she was unable to relax
and presently, realizing that she was getting chilled
and that it was time to take her dip, she reached for her
towel. She started to rise, half turning as she did so.

That was how she noticed the blur of movement
behind her. After that it happened so quickly that she
had no time to think. For there was no other warning
beyond the lingering uneasiness, intuitive or otherwise,
no sound beyond the surf and the crunch of sand she
made when she stood up.

One moment she was quite alone; the next she sensed
rather than felt the movement close beside her and
heard the paralyzing sound of breathing not her own.

Then the arms were reaching for her, finding her.

Hard bare arms, one clamping her shoulders and
yanking her backward while the other hand fell across
her face and pressed tightly against her mouth and nose.

The jerk of her head as she tried to avoid that hand
was instinctive. She felt the scream rising in her throat
even as she tried to struggle and wondered if only she
could hear it. Then it was choked off and her face was
in a muscular vise and she could no longer breathe.

She felt herself being lifted clear of the ground. She
clawed desperately at that hand and felt her fingernail
break. She kicked both feet and then, suddenly, something struck the back of her neck and her senses foun-
dered into utter darkness. . . .

18

DAVE BARNUM waited for five minutes after Workman left the bungalow before he turned out the
lights. He was beginning to worry about the long-distance call, already more than a half hour late, and he
thought if he waited in darkness it would be assumed
that he had gone to bed, lessening his chances of being
bothered unless it was something important.

From that moment on the minutes dragged and the
impatience grew in him. He kept looking at his watch
and trying not to. He began to curse the telephone,
the company, and his friend in California. This went on
until he realized how futile and childish he was being
and then, gradually, he began to explore the unlit,
silent places of his mind and his impatience fell away.
In its place there came a stirring of fear.

For by now he had an idea who had killed Stinson.
The trouble was he could think of no concrete proof to
support his theory and there was too much else he could
not account for: facts which seemed to have no rela-
tion to the crime.

And so he sat there in the dark by the front window
and tried to think as he had been taught to think in
college, taking one point at a time, starting from something he knew to be true and following a line of supposi-
tion along its crooked, convoluted path until he had to
abandon that possibility and start afresh. The pattern
was there if he could find it and he was not discouraged
when it failed to materialize. Again and again the blank
wall came up in his thoughts to frustrate him, and in
the end it was the telephone call which gave him what
he needed and dropped the key pieces into their proper
places.

The ring which came so abruptly startled him. He

was peering out the window, watching Betty's unit, though he was not aware of it, and seeing her light go out. He could not see her door open but a moment later he saw someone moving and he could tell the figure wore a robe. Then he was jumping for the telephone and sweeping it up before its first shrill summons had ended.

"Hello," he said in hard, impatient tones. "What the hell took you so long?"

"I've been trying since seven thirty our time," his friend said. "They kept calling me back and telling me the circuits were still busy. You want to hear what I've got?"

After that Dave listened with only brief interruptions, for the pattern was unfolding in his mind even as he listened.

"Beverly Hills?" he said. "Yeah. . . . Yeah. That's right. In trust for ten years. And what's it amount to?" He listened, then said: "That must be the one. Yes, Elise. And what's that date again? April 19th?"

He thanked his friend and hung up. To help quiet the mental turmoil rising inside him he went outside, driven by a compulsion that was both excited and triumphant. Swinging round the corner of the bungalow, he crossed the drive and continued to the sandy slope where he stopped to let his eyes adjust themselves to the darkened landscape.

Almost at once he saw the white line of surf ahead of him and the limitless blackness beyond. Then, as he tried to locate Betty, he thought he heard the cry, a sudden, high-pitched note, not loud but distinct, and just as suddenly choked off.

The sound chilled him and he stood stock still, peering intently and listening again. Then, silhouetted against the breaking surf, he saw someone moving toward the water's edge.

He started to run, some new fear building swiftly amid his thoughts. He could tell, even at a distance, that there was something odd about the way the figure walked. It did not look like Betty and yet he knew she must be there.

He yelled then, calling against the night breeze. He saw the figure stop, and called again. This time he was heard, for suddenly he realized that what he had thought was a person was in reality two people, separating now, one bent over and sprinting along the beach and the other sinking inert and motionless to the sand.

After that, panic drove him forward because now, without yet knowing what had happened, he knew why.

Diagonally to the right a fleeing figure grew indistinct and shapeless in the night, but Dave kept straight on, afraid now to think or even to speculate until he reached the still figure on the sand and dropped down beside it.

"Betty!"

He slid one arm beneath the limp shoulders and his voice shook.

"Betty!"

He lifted her to a sitting position and took her face in his hand, holding her close while the thin line of the sea creamed in and died in the sand five feet away. He knew then that she was breathing, and he could see no mark of injury, and so he talked to her, not knowing what he said until she sighed and her lids fluttered. For a moment when her eyes opened there was only horror and suspicion in their depths. When he felt her stiffen he spoke quickly.

"It's all right, darling. It's all right."

She understood then. He saw the gleam of recognition. He felt the shudder run through her body and then she was clinging to him and he was lifting her in his arms, still talking as he carried her back to her robe and towel.

When they reached the dune she said she could stand up and he let her try, supporting her for another moment before he reached for the robe. When he held it for her he asked what had happened and she could not tell him.

"I don't know," she whispered. "I didn't see or hear a thing until he grabbed me. I don't know who it was. Some man. I tried to scream—"

"You did."

"I tried to wrench his hand from my face and I kicked and then something hit me on the back of the neck. That's all I can remember."

Dave looked back at the low-rolling surf as she spoke. He touched the back of her neck. There was no swelling here, and all he could think of then was that a sharp blow with the edge of the hand would bring unconsciousness to a woman like Betty, that it took very little water to drown a person. Some time later, perhaps in the morning, there would be a body on the beach, rolled there by the tide and surf. The verdict would be accidental drowning just as the night before it might have been a traffic accident.

The very thought of this sickened him until, presently, a healthy anger began to churn and spread through his chest, bringing with it a turn of mind that was at once logical and coldly calculating.

When they had walked slowly back to the motel's grounds he saw that there was only one light burning: in Stinson's apartment. The rest of the units were dark and quiet, and again the transients' cars filled the ports.

"Do you know who's in Stinson's place?" he asked.

"I thought it was a policeman."

A *policeman*, Dave thought bitterly. A policeman right on the premises. Less than an hour ago policemen all over the place and yet the attempt had been made. A gamble, boldly taken. A simple risk once the circumstances were known, prompted by a shrewd and calculating mind. It was luck, not the odds that spoiled it.

"Get dressed," he said. "I'll speak to the cop. And look, Baby." He took her hands in his after he had opened the door and turned on the light. "Stay here, please. Until I come for you. I'm going to get Workman too. I'm going to need some help."

When she closed the door he went across the lawn to Stinson's place and knocked. A man he had never seen opened the door and Dave asked if he was working for Captain Vaughn.

"See if you can get him on the phone," Dave said. "If you can't maybe the station can reach him on the radio but get hold of him some way. Tell him Dave Barnum wants to see him. It's important."

He turned without waiting for an answer, walked behind the office and the empty car-port which had been Stinson's. He stopped at the next one to strike a match and glance at the license plate, and then he recrossed the lawn to Workman's door. He knocked twice before the door opened and then Workman was looking out through the screen, a blinking, rumple-headed figure clad in pajamas.

"You'd better get dressed," Dave said. "Somebody tried to get Betty again."

"What?"

"Betty," Dave said patiently. "Someone tried to kill her on the beach."

"Tonight?"

"About ten minutes ago. We'll be at my place," Dave said. "There's a phone there and a bottle. I think she could probably use a drink."

Back at the bungalow he went to the telephone and asked for long-distance.

"I want to place two calls," he said and gave his name and number. "One to Tampa. I can't give you the number but I want the Gulf Drive-Urself and I'll speak to anyone there. . . . Also, I want to put in a person-to-person call to Mr. Willie Shear," he said and gave the address he knew. "If he's not there try to locate him. I'll take whichever call you get first."

Betty was dressed and waiting when he returned to her unit. She was still a little pale and her hazel eyes were uneasy even as she smiled at him. She kept glancing down at one hand as she made ready to leave, turning it palm up with fingers bent.

"Hurt yourself?" Dave asked.

"Broke a nail. When I tried to get away from him, I guess."

Dave took her arm. He said that Vaughn should be along after a while and until then they could wait at his place.

"I think," he said when they went inside, "that a drink for you might be in order."

"I think it might."

"For medical purposes," he added.

"Oh, of course." She smiled again to show she appreciated his attempt at humor.

He made the highball and then the telephone rang. He motioned her toward the corner chair.

"Just relax," he said, "and drink your drink like a good girl, and don't ask questions. . . . Hello," he said to the operator.

"Ready with Tampa. Go ahead, please."

"This is Sergeant Kelly of the Vantine police department," Dave said. "Just wanted to check on a car you rented a few days ago," he said, and gave the license number. "No . . . No trouble. Just want to check on the name and address of the person you rented the car to. . . . Yeah, sure." He waited, reaching for a pencil. When the information came he wrote it down.

Betty was watching him from her corner seat when he hung up. She was being a good girl. She was sipping her drink, her eyes full of questions, but making no sound. Two minutes later the telephone shrilled again.

"Hi, Kid," Willie Shear said. "You still having trouble?"

"Plenty," Dave said in the same conversational way. "I think maybe you can help me."

"I don't know why I should," Willie said, "but I'll listen. What's on your mind?"

"First off I want to tell you that this is a private con-

versation between you and me. No one's listening in.
No tape recorder's taking it down."

"That's interesting if true."

"I want to ask you some hypothetical questions,"
Dave said. "I want to put a hypothetical premise to you
and you can give me an answer based on the premise.
Is that clear?"

"I know what hypothetical means," Willie said, "if
that's what's worrying you."

"You were here the other night."

"Says you."

"Yeah. That's the hypothetical part. I've no way of
proving it since you had that little bonfire in your ash
tray"—he heard Willie chuckle—"but you know and I
know you were. You didn't know someone was going to
give me a Mickey or that John Gannon would be alone,
which means that either you were up this way and
decided to stop by to see if he'd signed that agreement
I'd drawn up, or you had a date with him, in which case
it wouldn't have mattered whether I was around or not
because John would have sent me into my room if he
didn't want me to know what was going on."

"That's quite a mouthful," Willie said, "but I'm still
with you. Let's say I had the date, hypothetically."

"So what I have to find out is how and why you got
that stack of bills and the agreement back."

"We could say John gave them to me."

"We could," Dave said, "but if we do it means he
was alive at that time. It means that one way or another
you'll have to stand a murder investigation whether it
can be proved or not."

"I see what you mean. That's a good answer." There
was a pause. "Okay. You tell it your way. I'll listen."

"In my premise John was dead when you got here.
You knew nothing about it. You hadn't been seen; you
could probably get out without being connected with
the murder. But there was this agreement, and for all
you knew, since I drew it up after you'd been here the
other day, it might have your name on it, which would

mean questions and possibly some suspicion. There were also five thousand bucks that belonged to you."

Dave took a breath and said: "Now that's not much money to you but still it's yours. And you know that when the safe is opened that money automatically becomes part of the estate. To get it you would have to prove it was yours and you had no receipt because while Gannon was alive you didn't need one. His word was good with you and you'd proved it by giving him the cash to prove you meant business. . . . Are you still listening?"

"Intently."

"All right. You know there's a good chance you'll never get the cash back, but you want it because it's yours and the deal is off. Now in my premise the outer safe door was open. If this were true, would you have taken the necessary few seconds to take the key to the inner door from Gannon's pocket and remove what was yours from the safe. Maybe it wasn't smart but the risk was small and being a gambler you took the chance."

"Wait a minute," Willie said. "I think I'm with you and your hypothetical reasoning bears out what I thought the other day: that you're a pretty smart youngster. But let's have the question again. Keep it simple."

"If you were there and saw a chance to get what was yours back with very little risk, would you have taken that chance?"

"Hypothetically, yes."

Dave let his breath out slowly, and with satisfaction. "Was the radio playing, Willie? Still hypothetically."

"Yes."

"You left it that way?"

Willie chuckled again. He said he would have left it that way if he had been there. Then, before Dave could hang up, he said:

"One thing more. If you ever get tired of that Boston office you've been slaving in give me a buzz. I can fix you up at twice the dough for half the work."

When Dave hung up, Betty's eyes were wide with wonderment and her half-full glass had been forgotten.

"What," she said bewilderedly, "was all that?"

Dave grinned at her. He said he'd tell her one day but right now it would be better if she forgot all about the conversation and kept her mind blank.

"On the advice of counsel?"

He nodded and then, hearing someone at the door, went over and opened it. Carl Workman came in clad in slacks, loafers, and a blue Oxford shirt. His thinning brown hair had been hastily combed and his amber eyes blinked as he stepped into the light. He glanced at Betty and then back at Dave. He asked if she was all right and Dave said she was.

"You call Vaughn?"

"He's on his way." . . .

19

CAPTAIN VAUGHN arrived before Dave could do more than give Workman the briefest outline of what had happened on the beach. There was another car behind Vaughn's and when Dave went outside he recognized Sam Resnik's sedan. Vaughn came to the door with the young officer named Steve.

"I hadn't finished with Sam," Vaughn said, "so I brought him and the girl along. The man that called in said you sounded like it was important."

"I think it is," Dave said.

"Good. The more important the better." Vaughn glanced at Resnik's car. "We could bring them in too."

It was not the way Dave planned it but he said all right and presently the living room was crowded. When everyone had found a seat but Steve, who leaned next to the door, Dave told what had happened to Betty.

When he finished, Resnik chuckled aloud, a surprising sound in view of what had happened. When Dave glanced at him the pale, mustached face was smooth and unworried.

"That was how long ago?" he said. "This beach thing?"

"About twenty minutes or a bit longer."

"For once"—Resnik gave Vaughn a look of veiled amusement—"I seem to be in the clear."

He exchanged glances with Liza Drake and hers was bright with approval. She leaned back in her chair, looking very striking in the clinging black gown that molded so effectively her full-breasted torso. She wore a comb in her shining black hair and carried a beaded evening bag; a mantilla-like shawl was draped over one bare shoulder.

"I believe we were with you twenty minutes ago, Captain," Resnik said.

Vaughn was not amused. His dark gaze was bleak and he took time to direct it at Resnik and then at Liza before he turned to Betty and began to question her. What he heard added nothing to what was already known and now he looked at Dave.

"This ties in with the murder, maybe?"

"Maybe."

"You got some ideas?"

"A few," Dave said, "but first there's something I have to know about. That's why I asked Carl to come over." He glanced at Workman, and then at Betty, who had put her glass aside and was watching him attentively. "It concerns you," he said, "but Carl has the answers."

Workman had been sitting with his legs crossed. Now he uncrossed them and leaned forward, brows warping in a frown.

"About what?"

"About the missing heir you're looking for. The daughter of Albert L. Colby, isn't she? Named Elise?"

"That's right."

Dave tipped one hand in a deprecating gesture. "The other afternoon I thought it might be Liza."

"Liza?"

"Me?" Liza sat up while an expression of bewilderment began to work on her features. "Me?" she said again.

"It was the name," Dave said. "Liza—Elise. Plus the fact that your father and mother had separated when you were young and you didn't know where your father was or anything about him. So I decided to see if I could check on Albert Colby's will." He looked at Workman.

"Somehow I had an idea that maybe this search of yours tied in, in some way, with the murder of John Gannon. I remembered I had a friend practicing in Los Angeles, a boy I'd gone to law school with. It was too late to call him yesterday when I first thought of it, but I got hold of him today. I told him what I wanted and he called me back tonight."

When no one spoke he said: "Elise is a form of Elizabeth." He looked at Betty, disturbed because he had to question her in front of the others but knowing no other way now. "Your name is Elise, isn't it?"

"I—I was christened Elise but"—she hesitated, the wonderment growing in her hazel eyes—"I've never used it. I've always been Betty as long as I can remember. My mother's name was Elizabeth and—"

Her voice trailed off as Dave turned back to Workman.

"Betty's right name is Elise Nelson Colby, isn't it?"

"No!" the girl protested. "Mother's name was Nelson."

"Yes," Dave said patiently. "Her maiden name. My guess—and that's all it is—is that she dropped the Colby and told you your father's name was Nelson. I think your father hired Workman before he died."

"No." She had her chin up now, her color rising. She looked quickly about the room as though in some plea for support from those who were listening. "My father died in a hotel fire when I was seven."

Dave saw her distress. He wanted to tell her he was
sorry and ask for her understanding. Workman paid
no attention to her denial. It was as if she were no longer
in the room, for now he was watching Dave, leaning
forward slightly, half-closing one eye.

"How did you tumble?" he asked quietly.

Dave took a small breath and the strain which had
been growing inside him eased slightly. Somewhere in
the room there was a stifled exclamation but he did not
glance round.

"Betty told me she was born in Jamaica Plain, Massachusetts, on April 19th, 1930. I remembered because I'm
from Boston and I know it's a local holiday. My lawyer
friend told me that the missing daughter identified in
Colby's will was born in the same place and on the
same date."

He swallowed and said: "Now it might be coincidence that two girls could have the same birthplace and
date and not be the same person. But it's asking too
much of coincidence to have you down here looking for
such a girl, and finding one that qualified by birth,
and then have her turn out to be someone else."

Workman grunted softly and there was a suggestion
of admiration in the sound. He seemed not at all per-
turbed and said: "That's nice figuring and I hope you're
right. I'll know for sure in a day or so."

"I don't believe it." Betty shook her head, her brown
hair flying. "My father is dead."

Workman looked at her. He took his time answering
and now his tone was blunt and impatient.

"Sure," he said, "but he didn't die when you were
seven and he didn't die in any hotel fire. That's what
your mother told you but I know different because I
worked for him. I can give you the other side. It'll take
a while but now that we're started you might as well
have it. . . . Okay with you, Captain? . . . Who's got
a cigarette?"

Vaughn nodded. There was a lot of thought in his
eyes but he had leaned back comfortably in his chair.

For a little while he was not a policeman pressing a murder investigation; he was an interested listener and his attitude suggested he had all the time in the world.

Dave supplied the cigarette and a light. Now Workman leaned back and drew smoke into his lungs. When he was ready he spoke slowly and with conviction.

"Some of this I got from your father," he said to the girl. "Some of it I dug up later, but this much is certain. Albert Colby's wife, Elizabeth, left him when their daughter Elise was seven years old. Colby was a salesman and he was away a lot and he and his wife didn't get along. The reason doesn't matter, and anyway all I know is his side. What does matter is that he came back from a ten-day trip one afternoon to find his wife and daughter gone."

He hesitated and said: "He never knew where they went or what happened. He knew your mother had an uncle out in Wisconsin but he didn't bother to check because he didn't particularly care at the time. There was only this rented house and the furniture and a car, which he used on his trips. He sold the furniture, packed his personal things, and moved out. Later he drifted out to the West Coast and he did pretty well financially. Five years ago he married a young divorcée. Last year he found out he was going to die. The doctors told him it was only a matter of months and that's where I came into the picture. He didn't know whether you or your mother were alive but he wanted to find out before he died. He especially wanted to find you. The trouble was he started too late and time ran out on him."

He reached over and jabbed the cigarette out. For another moment the room was still. Vaughn had not moved, nor had Resnik. Liza was sitting up attentively, a look of fascination on her face and her painted lips parted. Betty sat immobile and bewildered and Dave waited, wanting the rest of the story but afraid to interrupt.

"Before your father died he changed his will," Workman said. "That made it important for the lawyers handling the estate to find you if they could, and since I'd already started they kept me on. I've been on it altogether ten months," he said, "and it took me a long time to get a lead. If I had known in the beginning that your mother was a dressmaker it would have helped. She took you to New York, didn't she? And got a job in the garment industry."

"Yes."

"And they have strong unions and that's how I got my lead. I was looking for an Elizabeth Colby or Elizabeth Nelson—I knew that was your mother's maiden name—and I found three or four. One of them had studied stenography nights and got a job as a secretary, still in the garment business. Later she went to this college town while her daughter finished high school. Am I right so far?"

The girl nodded, saying nothing.

Workman glanced at Vaughn, his eyes intent. "The only thing that Albert Colby kept were two baby pictures, a snapshot taken when his daughter was six, and a water color she had made for him one birthday. On the back of that sheet were three very clear prints from her right hand, made when she had a bit of paint on her fingers. Colby still had the pictures and the drawing."

He looked back at the girl. "I know I'm right," he said. "A comparison of fingerprints will prove it to the lawyers even though one set was taken fifteen years ago." He paused and said: "I told you I'd worked on this for ten months. I've got some dough tied up in it. If I take you back with me I'll collect a nice bonus."

"But—I don't want to go back."

Workman brushed aside the remark. He said she did not have to stay. All she had to do was prove her identity and she could do as she liked.

Vaughn cleared his throat. He said it was quite a story.

"It's easy enough to check if you don't think it's the truth," Workman said.

Vaughn was watching Dave. "How does this tie in with the two murders, or doesn't it?"

"That's what had me licked," Dave said. "I thought it had to in some way but I couldn't figure how. I thought I knew who had killed Gannon and—"

"Oh, you did, hunh?" This time Vaughn was quickly sarcastic. "Maybe you've known it right along."

"No," Dave said patiently, "I didn't get the idea until early this evening. But I still couldn't get any answer until I got this call from my friend. I told you he checked the will."

Vaughn nodded, still suspicious.

"Betty's father left an estate of nearly six hundred thousand dollars. He left a third of that outright to his widow, a thirty-four-year-old divorcée. He left two-thirds to Betty, payable any time within ten years if she could be located. If Betty could not be found the widow would get that two-thirds in ten years. If proof could be furnished that Betty was no longer living the widow would get that two-thirds at once."

He hesitated, measuring his words so there would be no mistake.

"I think Workman wanted Betty out of the way," he said. "I think he was afraid to do the job deliberately because a check-back with the lawyers who hired him would turn up the will and maybe supply a motive."

Workman cut him off before he could finish.

"Are you nuts?" he said, his mouth suddenly mean and hard. "What the hell reason would I have for killing her?"

"So Colby's widow could collect without waiting that ten years. I think you made a deal with her."

"Wait a minute!"

This time it was Vaughn who interrupted. He sat up, looking from Dave to Workman, his dark eyes busy but still puzzled.

"You're saying Workman's the one who tried to force Miss Nelson's car off the road last night?"

"Yes."

"Can you prove it?"

"No."

"This thing tonight on the beach—"

"Workman missed last night," Dave cut in. "He tried again tonight when no one would have expected it. But for a bit of luck he would have managed it."

"Can you prove that?"

"Maybe." Dave looked back at Workman and saw nothing but hate and defiance in the amber eyes. Then because he had to take a chance, he mentally crossed his fingers and went ahead. "Betty broke a fingernail on the man who grabbed her," he said. "She was trying to claw his hand from her mouth. There's a good chance she scratched him; if so there'll be traces of blood and skin under her cuticle."

"You're guessing now," Vaughn said.

"Workman had a motive," Dave argued, "and until now I've never seen him wear anything but short-sleeved shirts." Still looking at Workman he said: "How come you're wearing an Oxford shirt with long sleeves now? Roll up your cuffs!"

"Captain." Workman appealed to Vaughn with a gesture that suggested the whole thing was ridiculous. "This guy is off his rocker. Do we have to sit here and listen to this sort of crap?"

"Watch your language. . . . Go ahead," he said, "roll up your sleeves! You've got nothing to hide."

"Like hell."

"Steve!"

The young officer by the door started for Workman. Vaughn got ready to rise. Dave stayed where he was, suddenly anxious because Workman made no move.

"Which arm would you say, Miss?" Vaughn asked.

Betty shook her head as though to clear it. At that moment she seemed to understand no part of what was going on but she finally managed an answer.

"The left, I think. Yes, the left."

Workman sat unmoving. He let Steve unbutton his cuff. When the sleeve was pulled up a three-inch scratch showed just above the wrist, the line of it red and raw looking.

"Ahh—" said Vaughn with a grunt of satisfaction. "Now we're getting somewhere." He looked at Dave. "And you're saying Workman wanted the girl out of the way because he made a deal with the widow. That makes sense but is it anything more than a hunch?"

"If it isn't," Dave said, "why would Albert Colby's widow arrive here yesterday and register under the name of Thelma Collins?"

"What?" Vaughn's face dissolved into a network of humps and wrinkles. "Here?"

"Number 3," Dave said.

"Are you sure?"

Dave said he was. He explained how he had been looking at Stinson's car that morning. He said he had looked at Thelma Collins's car and noticed that it was hired.

"Rented in Tampa," he said. "I phoned the place before you came. . . . To rent a car," he said, "you have to show your license, which has your name and home address on it. There's a record of it. The woman who rented that car and registered here as Thelma Collins had a California license bearing the name of Thelma Colby."

Captain Vaughn had heard enough. He looked real pleased. He asked Workman what he had to say and when there was no reply he turned to Steve.

"Number 3, Steve," he said. "Give her time to get some clothes on but that don't mean time to fix her hair and paint her mouth. Get her over here."

20

STEVE HAD managed very well with Thelma Collins because he ushered her into the bungalow no more than five minutes later. She was wearing a gray slack-suit and she had a scarf bound round her auburn hair, but the lipstick she had applied so hurriedly gave her mouth a lopsided look and her face seemed strangely naked without its customary arc of eyebrow pencil.

She gave a very good performance of a highly indignant and outraged woman. Her glance slid to Workman as she entered but it moved on almost at once, as though looking for some victim. When she did not find one she said:

"Who's in charge here?"

Vaughn bowed from the neck up. "I am, Ma'am."

"Well, let me tell you something. I'm going to report this to your superiors. The idea of sending a policeman to my room at this hour and—and—"

She stalled, her momentum failing.

Vaughn said: "I don't have any superiors, except the mayor. I'm the acting boss. . . . Sit down, please, Ma'am."

Thelma decided to follow the suggestion. She found a place at the end of the settee. She looked again at Workman and now her green eyes said she was worried.

"First," Vaughn said, "I'd like to ask you why you registered here under a false name?"

"I beg your pardon?"

"You signed the register as Thelma Collins."

"That's my name."

"Not according to your driving license." Vaughn had the range now and he was taking over. "We," he said, using the editorial form, "checked with the people you rented that car from over in Tampa."

He explained how he knew these things and offered her a chance to produce the license and prove him wrong. When her glance flicked to Workman once again, Vaughn continued.

"We'd like the truth out of you, Ma'am. For all we know you may be innocently involved in this thing and we want to give you every chance."

"What thing?" Thelma swallowed, her nervousness

increasing. "I don't know what you're talking about."

"Mr. Workman's in trouble."

"Not much," Workman said nastily. "Tell them nothing," he said to the woman. "They can't do a thing to you if you clam up."

Vaughn ignored the remarks. "I'll tell you how much trouble Mr. Workman is in—just trouble that we know of. He'll be arrested for assault for one thing. The way he did it, in this state, would warrant a charge of attempted rape, not to mention assault with intent to kill. Now just how you make out depends on a lot of things."

"But"—the woman looked frantically about and her voice broke—"but I don't know what you mean."

Vaughn studied her, as though trying to discover how much of this demonstration he could believe. So did Dave. With no idea how deeply Thelma Collins—or Colby—was involved, he got the impression she really meant what she said. He found himself hoping this was so.

"Did you know," Vaughn said, "that this young lady you know as Miss Nelson is actually Miss Colby, your late husband's daughter?"

Thelma went white. "I don't believe it."

"Just take my word for it," Vaughn said. "She's Mr. Colby's daughter and Mr. Workman twice tried to kill her." He leaned forward, his tone suddenly brusque. "Why did you come to Florida, Mrs. Colby?"

"Why"—she glanced uncertainly at Workman—"he asked me to come."

"From California? How? Phone you? Wire?"

"He telephoned me the first of the week."

"What exactly did he say?"

"He said I was to fly here as soon as I could, and go to some hotel in St. Petersburg or Tampa and to wire him from there."

"What reason did he give you for all that?"

"He said it was about the estate."

Vaughn nodded. "All right. You got over there in

Tampa and you wired him where you were. Then what?"

"He called me. He said to rent a car and drive over here and register under an assumed name. He said it was important that no one know who I was and that he'd explain when he saw me."

"What was the explanation he gave you?" Vaughn asked. When she hesitated he said: "Did he make you some sort of proposition regarding your share of the estate?"

"Don't be a fool!" It was Workman, his tone clipped and commanding. "They can't make you talk."

"He's right," Vaughn said, holding the woman's attention with his dark gaze. "In this country nobody can make anybody talk if he don't want to. But this I can tell you, Mrs. Colby. Workman's going to jail. Tonight. Whether you go with him—"

"They can't hold you," Workman said, still appealing to the woman.

"I don't say we can," Vaughn said, answering, but to her. "But you'll spend the night in a cell so you'll have a chance to think things over. If you want to stay here tonight you'd better keep on talking. . . . Now, did Workman make you a proposition?"

Thelma was holding her hands breast high, twisting her fingers unconsciously. She began to chew the red paint off her lips.

"Yes," she said in a voice of desperation.

Vaughn glanced at Dave and gave him a small nod of confirmation. He leaned back again and his tone moderated.

"All right, Mrs. Colby. Now just tell us what it was Workman proposed to do. Take your time. Tell it in your own words."

Thelma made up her mind. Dave could see it from the way she set her jaw and put her head up. From now on she would be thinking of Thelma and what was good for Thelma.

"He said he had a line on Mr. Colby's daughter. He said there was a chance that she was dead but that it would take a lot of work for him to prove it. He said it might be expensive. He said he felt he was entitled to a share of the rest of the estate if he could get it for me soon."

"And what did you say?"

"I asked him what he meant. I didn't understand him at first."

"And he told you," Vaughn said, "that if he let the matter drop and said nothing, if this girl who might be dead was not identified, you'd have to wait nearly ten years for the balance of the estate."

"Yes."

"Well, what did he want? What did he propose to do?"

"He asked me if I would give him twenty per cent of what I got in case he could get the rest of the estate for me."

"He didn't tell you that the way he was going to do that was to kill the girl the estate belonged to?"

"Oh, God, no!" she cried in a voice so genuinely distressed that Dave was ready to believe her. "He said the girl was dead but he wanted to be paid for proving it. He said did I want my money now enough to give him a percentage or did I want to wait."

"You said you wanted it now?"

"Well—yes. Naturally I—I mean, I thought it was worth it—"

When she let the sentence hang Vaughn said: "Was there some agreement between you? Anything on paper?"

"Yes. We went to Orlando yesterday after I came. He had the agreement notarized."

"You have a copy? . . . We'll want to see it but for now just tell me what it said."

"It said that I agreed to give him twenty per cent of any money I collected from my husband's estate provided I collected within one year."

Vaughn rubbed his hands and allowed himself a

smile. He looked at Workman, still smiling but contempt in his eyes.

"That," he said, "makes a right smart motive. . . . Thank you," he said to the woman. "We won't bother you any more tonight."

She seemed not to understand and made no move to rise. "You mean I can go?"

"For tonight, yes, Ma'am. In the morning you'll come down to my office and put what you've told me in writing. I don't think there'll be any charges."

He stood up when she did, walked with her to the door and opened it for her. Then, when she had gone, he looked at Workman.

"Twenty per cent, eh?" he said disgustedly. "Eighty thousand bucks. You want to tell us the rest of it?"

Workman had been a policeman and he knew the value of silence. No man could legally be made to talk against his will and he intended to make the most of it. The exasperation on his hard-jawed face was sullen but challenging. He sat where he was and said nothing at all. Even when Vaughn told Steve to put the handcuffs on, Workman made no sound, nor did he move until he was told to stand up.

"Take him down, Steve," Vaughn said. "You know where to put him. Then come back here."

21

WHEN THE screen door closed and Captain Vaughn turned to look the room over, his glance stopped on Betty. For the past few minutes she had sat silently in her corner chair, looking small and alone and bewildered by what was going on about her. Dave, torn inside by her distress and wanting more than anything to do something to help her, had been forced to stay where he was. To say anything now, to indicate how

he felt in front of the others would only embarrass her
and he was grateful now when the captain spoke to
her.

"I know this has been a real shock to you, Miss Nelson
—I guess you're still Miss Nelson to me," he said kindly.
"But now that you know the truth wouldn't you like
to go back to your room and try to get some rest?"

Betty did not hesitate. She shook her head. She looked
at Dave and tried to smile, as though to prove she was
all right. It seemed to him then that what she was afraid
of was being alone but what she said was:

"Oh, no. I—I'd rather not just yet."

Vaughn nodded and a small sigh escaped him. He
seemed almost reluctant to get on with his investigation.
He looked at Resnik sitting there impassively in his
white jacket, at Liza Drake who sat beside him. Finally
he got around to Dave.

"Thanks for the assist," he said frankly. "Narrows
things down, I guess."

"It was the phone call," Dave said. "The work my
friend did on checking the will."

"You had to think to ask him first though." Vaughn
walked to the door and came back. "How does that tie
in with the murder?"

"I don't know that it does. That's what confused me.
I was worried about Betty. She saw Sam outside here
the night Gannon was killed—"

"That's still only *her* story," Resnik said to break his
long silence.

Dave ignored the interruption and continued to
Vaughn.

"When I understood Workman's possible motive for
wanting"—he glanced at Betty but had to finish the
thought—"Betty out of the way, I tried to find a motive
for shooting Gannon. The only thing I could think of
was that he might have killed Gannon, without motive,
on the assumption that having no motive he would not
be a suspect unless caught in the act. That way if anything happened to Betty you'd assume the same man

did both jobs and Workman, having no motive on the first, would have none on the second."

Vaughn nodded. He said he could see what Dave meant. "But it's not very good," he added.

"No," Dave said, "it isn't. I don't think Workman had anything to do with Gannon's death. Workman was an opportunist and when Gannon was killed I think he worked on the theory I've just outlined. He didn't kill Gannon but he saw a chance to kill Betty—" He looked at her again, distressed by what he was saying.

"Yeah," Vaughn said. "If an accident happened to her so much the better. If it looked like murder we'd think the same one did it that killed Gannon."

"He'd been working on the job for ten months, on a bonus arrangement," Dave said. "He finally found what he was looking for but he'd spent a lot of money on expenses and it occurred to him that it wasn't enough. He was smart enough to figure out a way. Instead of winding up with a couple of thousand legitimately he saw a chance to collect about eighty thousand, probably more than he ever dreamed of."

"A guy like him," Vaughn said, "yes."

"The report you got on him said he was a tough, ambitious cop. He'd killed, or at least shot, two kids with a stolen car. He was a callous, greedy guy who was ready to do what he had to do without compunction. Eighty thousand was motive enough for Workman."

"Nicer guys than him have killed for less, a lot less," Vaughn said. "He was a wrongie. Mean. He had the look." He hesitated and brought his mind back to the subject at hand. "But he didn't kill Gannon or Stinson."

"No," Dave said, "he didn't. He couldn't have. He had an alibi with Gannon but I didn't know about that until tonight."

Vaughn's eyes narrowed. "Oh, yes," he said slowly. "You mentioned something about knowing who did it."

"I can tell you who didn't do it."

"Prove it, can you?"

"Not with evidence that would stand up in court but I think I can prove it to you."

"Try."

Dave considered the things he had to say and tried to arrange them in the proper order in his mind. He felt sure he was right but the tension was working on him now, coming not from apprehension but from the strain that had been mounting within him. He was conscious of the hot stillness of the room as he hesitated, the stickiness of his clothes. He took a short breath and stepped over to the radio. He pointed to the dial. Vaughn stepped up to have a look.

"This thing is set for station WTCX," Dave said. "You can take my word for it or you can turn it on and wait for a station break."

"Go ahead," Vaughn said. "What makes it important?"

"John Gannon had funny radio habits. He wanted one wherever he was, for the news, and for racing results. He used to run some handbooks. He's always been interested in horses and nearly every day he had a bet down somewhere."

"I remember the parlay slip we found in his pocket," Vaughn nodded. "I checked it. The second horse ran out of the money."

"Since we were here," Dave said, "he listened to two stations only. For all he cared you could have taken the rest of them off the air. At noon—when he was here—and at six o'clock always, he listened to the news on WTCX. Always at eleven fifteen he tuned in WCXM to get the racing results. He made a point of being here; he never missed since we arrived."

He swallowed and said: "Gannon listened to the WTCX news before dinner on the night he was killed. When I came in from the Club 80 and found him dead the radio was playing dance music. When I came back with Betty and Workman after chasing whoever it was that slugged me"—he looked at Resnik but decided not to accuse him then—"it was still playing. Is that right, Betty?" he said to the girl.

"Yes," she said. "I remember."

"I turned it off before I phoned the police. I didn't
notice the station then but before that I remembered a
disc-jockey saying that this was station WTCX."

"I remember too." Betty was sitting up now, interest
stirring in her hazel eyes. "You turned it off before the
man finished."

"The next noon I was here," Dave continued. "I turned
on the news like Gannon used to do. I didn't have to
tune a station in to get it. It was already on WTCX."
He shrugged. "I didn't think anything about it. I didn't
think anything about it until tonight. At six o'clock I
turned the radio on again. I hadn't touched the dial
since the murder. But I was doing some thinking by
that time and all of a sudden it hit me."

Vaughn hadn't quite caught up. He scowled. "What
hit you?" he demanded.

"The idea that we'd been figuring wrong about our
times. Because if Gannon had been alive at eleven fifteen the radio would have been tuned to station WCXM
for the racing results. If it had been then turned off
after that, and later turned back on by the killer to
cover the shot, it would still have been on WCXM. The
killer wouldn't care a damn what station he had so long
as there was noise. It certainly would not have been on
WTCX unless it had already been set for that station.
To me that proves that Gannon died before eleven fifteen."

He hesitated, perspiring freely now and a little out of
breath. He watched Vaughn, seeing the unspoken
agreement in the other's weathered face.

"You've got a timetable," he said. "Most of what you
have has been corroborated. You know where people
were and when they got here."

"Resnik?" It was a question that Vaughn was asking.

Dave shook his head. "Between a quarter of eleven
and a quarter after Sam was at the club worrying about
a drunk who came close to breaking the bank. . . . No.
Check your list and you'll find that only two people

were here before eleven fifteen. George Stinson was
one. He was here all evening."

"Well," Vaughn said impatiently, "who was the other.
Tyler?"

Dave shook his head again. "The only other person
who could have done it is the one who brought him
here." Then, not mentioning her name, he looked at
Liza Drake.

22

ONCE AGAIN the room was still. The heat seemed to
settle like the silence, gathering tension as it fell. Liza
Drake's shawl had slipped from the bare shoulder to her
lap. Her face was composed but oddly pale around the
cheekbones and her red lips held a funny little smile.

"That's silly," she said and her laugh, though not loud,
had a harsh, artificial sound. "That's not even funny."

"Wait a minute!"

Resnik demanded attention but he did not get it from
the woman.

"Me shoot Mr. Gannon?" she said. "How crazy can
you get?"

Resnik tried again. His hooded eyes were bright and
unpleasant and his little mustache seemed to flatten
against his teeth.

"This is nothing but a lousy frame," he said. "You
haven't got a thing . . . What the hell does the radio
prove?" he demanded, glaring at Dave. "You could have
set it anywhere you wanted to. As evidence it isn't
worth fifteen cents and you know it."

Dave made no attempt to answer the argument because he knew it was sound. Instead he continued to
talk to Vaughn as though there had been no interruption, wanting to get across the things he had in his mind,

the few that were facts, the others that he could not prove even though he knew them to be true.

"She was the obvious one all along," he said. "It was so simple we overlooked it entirely. At least I did," he added in a voice that indicated how disgusted he was with himself.

"She had the sleeping capsules. She knew, with Betty there, that I'd dance with her. She could be alone in that corner booth. She had all the time in the world to fix up my drink and when it worked I have an idea she called it to Gannon's attention, knowing it might appeal to his sense of humor. It did. He fell for it and she offered to drive him home, with a gun in her bag."

"Nuts!" Resnik said, half shouting now.

"She came in with him," Dave said. "For some reason he opened the safe. Whether she intended to kill him anyway or whether he stalled her somehow and made a move to get the gun I don't know."

"I'll say you don't," Resnik said. "Guesses. Nothing but guesses, none of which you can prove. . . . Look, Captain," he said, his voice steadying as he appealed for attention. "To kill a person you've got to have a motive. Even a lunatic must *think* he has a reason. I knew Gannon quite a while. If anybody had a motive, I did. Liza knew him about a week. She was never alone with him, hardly knew him. Why? Why should she want to kill him?"

Vaughn opened his mouth as though about to speak and then closed it, his frown perplexed. When he had given the matter a second's thought he answered.

"This is Barnum's idea," he said to Resnik. "Suppose we let him tell it." He looked at Dave. "You got an answer?"

"I've got a motive. An obvious one if you'll stop and think about it."

He hesitated, knowing he was right but not knowing exactly how to say so. It was a hard thing for him to attempt because he was young. It made him self-conscious when he tried to find the right words. He started by asking Vaughn a question.

"In your experience what would you say was the best murder motive for a woman?"

Vaughn had to think it over and it gave him a little trouble. "Wouldn't know for sure. I'd say jealousy."

"Love," Dave said.

"What?"

"Love, with its associated emotions like jealousy and hate."

"Okay."

"That's the motive," Dave said, and then he was talking, remembering what he knew about Liza Drake, the impression she had made on him that other afternoon, the things she had said. He did not stop to think about the continuity or progression of his words, he simply spoke them as they came. He told of Liza's background and the struggle she'd had to get anywhere as a singer. He repeated her own evaluation of her voice and her future.

"All that time," he said, "she knew what she wanted: the right man. She'd seen all kinds and had to deal with them, one way or another. It took her quite a while but she knew her subject matter and finally she found him."

"Sam," Vaughn said.

"Now wait a minute," Resnik said again.

"You keep still!" Vaughn said. "You asked the question; now listen to his answer. You'll get your turn later."

"She's wearing his ring," Dave said. "From things she told me the other day my guess is that she would have married him on any terms. He didn't want it that way because he happened to be just as much in love with her." He looked at Resnik and said: "You told me that tonight and what you did about Tyler would seem to prove it. I can tell that if I have to."

This time Resnik was quiet. His naturally pale face had begun to tighten across the cheekbones and his narrowed gaze was intent.

"Sam," Dave continued to Vaughn, "was worried about the agreement with Gannon. He knew Gannon was thinking of selling to Willie Shear for a price Sam couldn't meet."

Still talking steadily and not bothering with the effect he was creating, he digressed to explain Willie Shear's luck which took the twenty-two thousand from Resnik and ruined his chances of buying the club. He explained the terms of the agreement.

"The way things stood," he said, "Sam had worked three years to build up a profitable business and all he was going to get out of it was a few thousand dollars' worth of furniture and gambling equipment he might not even be able to sell. That's how it stood with Gannon alive. That way Sam was out in the street while Willie Shear took over. With Gannon dead Sam was, and is, in business."

"So what?" Resnik said, interrupting. "That's my motive, not Liza's."

"Sure," Dave argued. "But you're a gambler and you've had bad breaks before and learned to accept them. Gannon's deal was legitimate and you had to take it. With Liza it was different. You'd planned to be married before Gannon decided to do business with Willie. Either you told her the marriage would have to wait until you had a stake again, or she assumed it. In you she had what she'd dreamed of having all her life. She didn't intend to lose out."

He paused, his throat dry and the strain working on him again. He said: "She didn't want any postponement, not after waiting that long. Maybe she was afraid a postponement would turn out to be no marriage at all. And one man was spoiling everything for her. Gannon. It was his fault and she knew you would do nothing about it. If anyone was to stop Gannon it would have to be her, and once she made up her mind she knew what she had to do. She did stop him. Maybe you didn't know it before but you know it now."

He turned to Vaughn. "She did it. She stopped him

in the only way she knew. She drove him home with a
gun in her bag and she went inside with him and she
shot him. Maybe she'll tell us what went on in that room
and maybe she won't but that's what happened. Then
she walked out and ran into George Stinson . . . I can
guess about that too if you want me to," he said.

"Go ahead," Vaughn said. "We got time."

"Sure," Resnik added. "Anybody can guess."

Dave looked at Liza; something had gone out of her
face, leaving it inert and lifeless. There was a slackness
about the full mouth but the eyes were dead. He did
not think he would get an answer, but he asked her anyway, asked her when Stinson had seen her, and whether
he knew at the time what she had done or not until
later.

Resnik said: "Don't answer that!" but the warning
was unnecessary. She seemed not even to hear what
Dave said.

"I think Stinson was quiet in the beginning because
she had done him a favor too by killing Gannon," he
added. "Like Liza, Stinson had one thing he wanted
above everything else. She wanted her man and he
wanted a little business of his own. It didn't matter if
the Villa Greer wasn't much of a motel. When Stinson
finished with it, it would shine because he had plans and
imagination, and he wasn't afraid of hard work.

"A fellow named Tyler walked in," he said, "and in
trying to hurt him, Gannon put Stinson on the spot.
Gannon may have said he'd make it up and he may not
have. In any case there was nothing Stinson could
count on. Then Gannon is killed and, like that, Stinson
has what he's always wanted. He couldn't wait to
call the owner and tell him he was ready to take an
option."

Vaughn cleared his throat. "I checked. He phoned
after we'd left that night."

"You scared him yesterday," Dave said.

"Plenty."

"I scared him too. I was checking his car for dents

and I told him you were seeing Greer about that option. Stinson already had a guilty conscience. He'd kept still about Liza and now he was afraid for himself. He thought he'd have to tell the truth to protect himself and he made the mistake of warning her first. I guess he was that kind of guy. Tell her first, give her a chance to run for it. . . . Who knows what he thought, but that's what he did."

Watching the woman now but still talking to Vaughn, he said: "You spoke about a man having trouble coming up the beach and hiding a gun. Liza had a beach bag. Most women do when they go to the beach. She was a regular at that beach, and anyway, no one would think twice about a woman walking along with her beach bag. Then up the bluff to the road where Stinson was waiting in the car, talking to him a moment and finding out she couldn't trust him any longer. Maybe the second murder doesn't matter after the first," he said wearily. "Maybe you're a different person."

He let the words trail off, out of breath now and feeling all used up inside, feeling his shoulders sag and finding nothing more to say.

Then Resnik laughed.

It was a short, abrupt sound, carrying a connotation of contempt. But Resnik did not look contemptuous. His gambler's face was gray, the little mustache appearing now as a bizarre appendage. The eyes gave him away too, for they were no longer gambler's eyes, they were the eyes of a man who had been stricken by some unexpected force he could not handle. Now, having heard the truth and recognized it as such, he cast it away from him.

"You tell a hell of a story," he said, "but you can't prove a nickel's worth."

Vaughn walked over to the door again and came back, his weathered face distressed and full of thought.

"Can you?" he asked finally.

"No," Dave said. "I'm no cop. I'm not the judge, the jury, or the prosecutor. I had no idea Liza was coming here. I intended to tell you what I knew and that would be that. The rest of it's up to you. I was worried about Betty. Now nothing's going to bother her. That's all I want."

He dropped down on a chair, feeling discouraged and defeated, yet somehow reluctant to quit. That was how he thought of this final point.

"After Liza shot Gannon she kept the gun," he said. "She couldn't have known then that Stinson was going to see anything but she kept it. She used it again. If she carried it in her beach bag an analysis might show a trace of oil or grease, something to indicate a gun had been carried there."

He glanced up, not hopefully but still trying. "She might still have it. You could hold her while you went over her apartment. There's a chance—"

"You want a gun?"

It was Liza. She spoke in a voice that was leaden and without inflection. The slackness was still pulling at her mouth. She seemed not to have moved but when Dave looked at her he saw the gun in her hand, moving out from beneath the shawl.

"I'll give you a gun," she said, but that was not what she meant. For she was not handing anyone a gun. She was pointing it right at Dave, a Mauser, as Vaughn had guessed, small, compact, with a polished wooden grip.

23

WHAT SCARED Dave the most then was not the gun, or that it was pointed at him, but the expression on Liza Drake's face, the glazed, unblinking look in her dark eyes. For it seemed now that there was no longer any intelligence or reason motivating her actions and he could not tell what she was going to do. When someone spoke he glanced up to discover it was Resnik.

Resnik, sitting two feet to one side of the woman, had turned stiffly at the hips. His face was twisted with shock. Heretofore his mind had rejected the things that were said even though he must have sensed that they were true; now he understood beyond all doubt that the woman he loved had killed because of him. He tried to help her, battling against the hopelessness that showed in his eyes.

"Liza!" He spoke quietly, his voice hoarse. "That's not the way, Baby. We can beat this thing with smart lawyers."

Liza seemed not to hear him. She was watching Dave, her hand tight on the gun, and now Vaughn spoke up to get her attention. He stood about six feet away from her, his face impassive, his voice sounding calm and unworried.

"That's good advice, Ma'am. Put that little gun back where it came from and take your chances in court."

Liza looked at him. She moved the muzzle his way. "Sit down, Mr. Vaughn," she said.

Vaughn considered the order and he was a pretty smart operator when it came to matters he understood. To Dave's surprise he obeyed, and then Dave knew why.

"All right." Vaughn eased down on the edge of a chair. "You want to talk about it some first?"

"Mr. Gannon was a nasty old man."

"Don't!" Resnik said, his voice anguished. "Liza!"

He might just as well have not been in the room.

"He was going to take Sam's business away," she said in the same flat monotone. "Sam built it up and Mr. Gannon wouldn't even give him a chance to keep it."

"I guess that meant you might not be getting married," Vaughn prompted.

She was not listening. She had some idea of her own in mind and she was going to carry on with it.

"I knew how to get him alone," she said. "I drove him home and I went inside with him and I had this gun. I told him I was going to kill him if he ruined Sam. It scared him. He knew I meant it. He said I mustn't shoot. He said he would fix it. There was a paper in the safe and he would sign it right then and everything would be all right."

She wet her lips and said: "He never meant to sign anything. He thought he could trick me but he couldn't. He opened the safe and I was behind him—"

"Liza!" Resnik tried again to get her attention but it was like arguing with a child who refuses to listen.

"He reached for those keys in his pocket," she said, "and then he tried to turn and grab for the gun. He wasn't quick enough and he wasn't as smart as he thought he was—or maybe he was too smart. He staggered back and reached for the chair. He sat down in it and leaned back and then he didn't move."

For perhaps five seconds the room was quiet again and then Vaughn put another question in that same easy way of his.

"You ran into George Stinson when you came out?"

Resnik had given up protesting. He sat motionless and attentive, as though held by some strange fascination he could not combat. Dave shifted his weight and thereby moved a few inches closer to the gun. He had no plan, could make none because he had no way of telling what the woman might do. But even as the tension began to move up the back of his legs he wanted to be ready if the chance presented itself. He stole a glance at Betty but she sat as though transfixed, her attention on Liza.

"Yes. He hadn't heard the shot but I knew he'd find out what had happened. I didn't dare shoot him then, out in the open like that, but I knew he'd tell the police about me. I had to do something."

"What was that?" Vaughn asked.

"I walked over to him. I said, 'I've just done you a big favor, Mr. Stinson. Please don't tell the police you saw me here until I've had a chance to talk to you.' Then I got back in the car and drove off."

When she hesitated Dave understood the boldness

and simplicity of her reasoning. Of all the things she might have said to Stinson she had picked the right one. She had done him a favor and she asked his co-operation. Stinson was the sort who would hurt no one deliberately, who would testify against a woman only with great reluctance, and even in that Liza had calculated correctly.

"I knew he hadn't said anything when the police didn't come for me that first night," she said. "I knew that if he had kept quiet that long he probably would stay that way. He would have," she said tonelessly, "if he hadn't scared so easily. I talked to him the next day," she said.

"I guess he suffered more than I did. I didn't think much about Mr. Gannon. I told myself it was his own fault and he'd got what was coming to him. Mr. Stinson knew he was doing wrong but he also knew I had done him a favor. He told me about the motel he was going to buy. He said maybe he'd always have it on his conscience but he'd help me if he could." She sighed unconsciously and lifted the muzzle of the gun which had begun to dip.

"Then today he called me and said he was afraid he was going to be arrested. I could tell he was afraid, all right, but I knew I'd have to talk to him to know for sure what he was going to do. I asked him to meet me and I took the gun in my beach bag. I liked Mr. Stinson," she said without emotion. "But I knew if you"— she nodded to Vaughn—"started to work on him he'd tell all he knew."

She shook her head as though to eradicate the thought but her eyes still held that glazed, remote expression.

"It didn't seem to matter," she said. "I didn't want to do it but it didn't seem to matter like the first time. I didn't want to go to prison. I'm not going to prison," she said. "That's why I kept the gun."

Vaughn had been listening attentively, nodding from time to time to indicate he understood how it was. Now he leaned slightly forward, his eyes on the gun. Then, before he could do anything more, Resnik made his move.

Dave did not see it start. He was watching Liza and wondering if he could reach her in case Vaughn started toward the gun.

All he actually saw was the blur of motion out of which a hand took shape. He heard Liza's cry of surprise. Then Resnik was twisting the gun down and away; in a continuation of the same movement he had it safely in his hand.

Vaughn's eyes opened and a glint of satisfaction flickered in them. He said: "Ahh." He put his hands on his knees as though to rise. "Thanks," he said, but he did not get up.

For something had happened to Resnik. His hopelessness of manner had vanished. His attitude was alert and purposeful and now, a tight, mirthless grin warping his little mustache, he reached inside that white dinner jacket. He pulled a short-barreled revolver from a shoulder holster and pointed it at Vaughn.

"Sit still, Captain!" he said. "Just take it easy."

24

IT WAS Liza Drake who gave the first audible reaction. She made a small cry of bewilderment and stared down at her bruised fingers. Resnik paid her no attention. Still intent on Vaughn, he fumbled with the small automatic until he had the clip free.

He began to thumb the shells out on the couch. There were four. He put the clip back and then spoke to Liza from the corner of his mouth.

"You understand this thing? You know how to get that other shell out of the chamber?"

She said yes and he handed it to her. She pulled back

the slide and the last bullet spun to the floor. When she stooped to get it he stopped her.

"Let it lay. It don't matter."

"You hurt my hand," she said. "Why did you have to—"

"Because I don't want you shooting anybody else. Now listen to me."

He paused and she watched him, the slackness still in her face, and it came to Dave then that there was very little left of the woman he had talked with the other afternoon. That woman had been shrewd and calculating, a possessive woman with great assurance and a highly developed protective instinct, ready and willing to do whatever she had to do to protect the man she loved. This woman seemed stunned and incapable of aggressive action. Even her body seemed to have sagged within the boned supports of the strapless dress.

Resnik spoke curtly in his effort to impress upon her mind what she was to do.

"They've got nothing on you except that gun," he said. "All this talk doesn't mean a thing. You can repudiate the whole damn business and make them prove it. Now get out of here. Take that gun with you. Go down to the beach. Walk either up or down, it doesn't matter, and throw that gun farther into the ocean than you've ever thrown anything in your life. You understand?"

Liza stood up, the little automatic hanging limply in her hand. She began to move slowly toward the door. Vaughn was watching Resnik. His hands were still on his knees.

"You think I'm going to let her get away with it, Sam?" he asked quietly.

"I have to try," Resnik said.

"It's like this," Vaughn said. "When I first joined the force I had to settle some things in my mind. I had to figure that if I kept at it there was a good chance that some fool would take a shot at me. I had to figure it could happen more than once and that maybe I'd get hit. In this business it's a chance you have to take, like an occupational hazard, and what you hope is, if you get hit, you don't get stopped for good."

He leaned forward another inch, a glance at the woman telling him she was two steps from the door. He did not look nervous or worried and nothing showed in his voice.

"So far I've been lucky," he said, "and if this is the time I have to buck the odds, why that's what I'm getting paid for. Now I'm going to get out of this chair and I'm either coming for you or I'm going after the woman. I haven't made up my mind yet which it will be. I just want to tell you now that this is a sucker play, Sam, because you can't win."

"You can't win 'em all anyway." Resnik's face was a flat, hard mask but his voice was steady. "But when somebody goes to bat for me I like to do the same for him. Liza made a mistake but she did it for me. It ain't a question of right or wrong. I have to play it the way I see it. I have to give her the chance. If I have to pay, okay."

"With your life?" Vaughn asked. "Because that's how it will be if you pull the trigger, and you know it."

"No." Resnik shook his head. "When you kill a man you're betting with your life. I've never done that yet and I'm not going to start now. But I'm pretty handy with this thing and if you reach for your gun I think I can wing you. Come for me and you'll have to take it in the leg. Five minutes," he said. "That's all I want."

"Just long enough for the sand to cover the gun so we'll never find it."

Vaughn stood up slowly as the screen door banged. He looked at it a moment, still not too concerned. He looked at Resnik and took his first step.

"I have to call you, Sam. You're going to jail anyway you look at it."

"I have to give her the chance. Maybe I'll have to take a few years but I can do that much standing on my head."

Resnik swallowed visibly. He lowered the muzzle of the gun slightly, the perspiration glistening on his face. Vaughn stopped, head slightly cocked, as though listening for something and then, with all that pressure building up, Dave opened his mouth to speak. He did not know what he was going to say but he had to say something. He had to make a move of some kind, to attract Resnik's attention in some way so that Vaughn would have a chance. In that same instant Vaughn turned his back on the gambler.

What happened then took Dave a moment to understand. For the sound came from outside and close by the bungalow windows. He heard the man's voice first, followed by the woman's startled cry, not loud but abrupt and as quickly still. He thought he could hear the sound of a brief scuffle and then there was silence.

Vaughn smiled slowly and did not bother to turn round.

"You're lucky, Sam," he said over his shoulder. "In my business you learn never to operate alone if you can help it. I've had a man outside ever since I came here. I thought he could handle it but I couldn't have waited much longer."

Resnik examined the gun in his hand and the expression that crossed his face was hard to define. Relief came as the stiffness slid away but with it there came a look that was forlorn and miserable and utterly defeated. He lifted his shoulders and took a deep breath. He tossed the gun six inches in the air and caught it in his palm, the butt reversed.

"She had a break coming," he said. "After what she did for me I had to give her her chance if I could."

He swung his arm down and up, tossing the gun in an easy arc to Vaughn who caught it neatly. Then he sat down on the couch and buried his face in his hands.

It was after two o'clock when Dave and Betty left the bungalow and it was nearly six when the police car brought them back. They got out at the office and walked across the lawn in the early morning light, exhausted physically and emotionally from the ordeal they had been through, first in Vaughn's office and later answering questions and making statements for the state attorney. They did not see Liza or Resnik after they left Vaughn's office and they saw nothing at all of Carl Workman. Now, silently and as if by mutual consent, they sat down on Betty's steps, their shoulders touching.

He offered a cigarette, and she took it and a light. At that moment there seemed to be nothing that either could say and Dave's glance moved idly along the rows of units. In the apartment next to Betty's, Mrs. Craft would be getting ready to wake up for another day of observation on the frailties of others. Next to her Frank Tyler, the catalyst who had started things even though he had no part in the murder, would be sleeping. The next apartment, Workman's, was empty and would presently be vacant.

The cars parked beside the two bungalows flanking Gannon's were ready and waiting to go and light showed in one of the windows, indicating that at least one tenant was making preparations for the day's journey. The three units diagonally opposite were still quiet and the fourth, the one next to Stinson's, was Thelma Colby's—Workman's Widow Collins. Dave wondered if her sleep had been troubled by thoughts of the estate she had wanted so badly, and if she realized how narrowly she had missed being an accessory, at least technically, to murder. . . .

"I'm sorry," he said, aware that Betty had spoken.

"I said, what will they do to her?"

"I don't know."

"Will—will they—"

"It depends on what her lawyers think of her chances. I think the least she'll get is a long term in jail."

"She deserves it," she said without vindication. "I can't feel too sorry for her. I think I feel sorriest for—"

"Stinson?"

"Well—yes. But I guess I was thinking of Mr. Resnik. She did it for him and now—"

She did not finish the thought but Dave knew what she meant: that it was the dead you mourned but the living you felt sorry for. He glanced away and now he saw through the trees the sunlight dancing on the water. He looked over at the light burning in the Coffee Shop and knew it would soon open for business. That gave him the idea.

"What time does it open?" he asked.

"At seven," she said, following his glance.

"What time is the coffee ready?"

"About a quarter of." She sighed. "Which means it's almost time for me to go to work."

"You've got time for a swim," he said. "Then we could have some of that coffee, couldn't we?"

"Why not? You're the boss."

"The boss?" he said, and then realized that this was so. He was the boss and it was time to think about what he was going to do about the Seabeach Motel. "Yes," he said. "I'm the boss and you're an heiress."

"Let's not talk about it. Ever."

He knew that the "it" she referred to meant the events of the past three days. He knew there would be times throughout the years when they would talk about them but they did not have to talk about them now.

He stood up and pulled her with him. For the second time he kissed her, lightly as before, without passion but with fondness and affection. When her hazel eyes smiled at him he told her to put her suit on; he said he would be waiting for her at the bungalow.

www.ingramcontent.com/pod-product-compliance
Lightning Source LLC
Chambersburg PA
CBHW020636180626
46816CB00003B/999